Rowdy Irish Tales for Children

The Arts Council
An Chomhairle Ealaíon

The Publishers gratefully acknowledge the financial assistance of The Arts Council/An Chomhairle Ealaíon

First published in 2001 by Mercier Press
5 French Church Street Cork
Tel: (021) 275040; Fax: (021) 274969
E-mail: books@mercier.ie
16 Hume Street Dublin 2
Tel: (01) 661 5299; Fax: (01) 661 8583
E-mail: books@marino.ie

Trade enquiries to CMD Distribution
55A Spruce Avenue
Stillorgan Industrial Park
Blackrock County Dublin
Tel: (01) 294 2556; Fax: (01) 294 2564
E.mail: cmd@columba.ie

© Edmund Lenihan 2001

ISBN 1 85635 366 4
10 9 8 7 6 5 4 3 2 1

A CIP record for this title is available
from the British Library

Cover design by Penhouse Design
Printed in Ireland by ColourBooks,
Baldoyle Industrial Estate, Dublin 13

Rowdy Irish Tales for Children

Eddie Lenihan

MERCIER PRESS

To Mary, the unsuspected listener

Contents

INTRODUCTION

What a strange thing it is that, in our modern Ireland of instant information and seemingly endless knowledge, the term 'storytelling' has come to be used so imprecisely. What the 'critics', as they set themselves up to be, rarely take into account is that there is a huge difference between storytelling and story-writing. And almost exclusively today in Ireland, what is available is story-writing.

Most of those who chatter about this subject have little or no experience of the oral variety of stories; they are 'literary' people, so they bring their prejudices to such discussion of the matter as occurs in the media. But whether they know it or not, there is a world of the spoken word – the told story – out there which still survives and for which Ireland is justly famous. This is the world I have called upon for the tales in this book. The two stories were originally told to my son Keith, 'The Brain-ball Factory' in May 1983 and 'The Wake of Carraig Clancy' in February 1984.

Making the transition from the spoken to the written word has been a challenge to me. How to preserve the freshness and immediacy of what is said and recreate it on the page? No easy task. For what is funny or tragic in words, accompanied by all the appropriate gestures of hand and face, may fall flat if merely transferred rigidly into print – which, after all, is a one-dimensional medium, depending much on the reader's mental agility and imagination.

Practically all of this is likely to be lost on present-day Irish critics, so I depend on children (though of every age, from nine to ninety!) to be the judges. If they find the voices and the situations real, then I will be more than satisfied. For I am confident that their reaction will be similar to that of him to whom the stories were first told: 'Yugh! That's disgusting . . . but tell me more. Pleeease!'

There will be more, never fear. And more . . . and more!

THE WAKE OF 'CARRAIG' CLANCY

In Ireland in the great, heroic days, it was the custom with nearly every family or clan, when a boy-child was born, to finger back carefully through the parchments of twenty-seven generations, and sometimes even nine generations further (just to be on the safe side), in order to find a name suitable to the newly born – one that would lend him stature in the eyes of those round about him. Names such as Eathal, Donnúir, Fearbhal, Mongán were nothing strange, or Gulaí, Ealtan, Lomhna, Achtán and Órlámh. And even Oghma, Urard, Caochar, Srugh, Iuchna, though odd, were still easily recognisable as good, traditional and Irish. They should, and usually did, sit comfortably on those they were bestowed on.

But there was an exception to the rule, as is usually the case. And it came from a quarter most unexpected: the bare west of Clare, an area called Corca Baiscinn.

In the fastnesses of that rushy place at that time, there lived a family by the name of Clancy. And no ordinary family, either. For one thing, they refused to acknowledge anyone as their superior, even the High King himself, and secondly, they put little or no value on the ancient Irish custom of the twenty-seven generations. Acting the fool, they called it. Mere eejiting. And they proved it, too – by the names they used for their own boys. Names such as Brutus, Augustus, Titus and so on.

This is how such a state of things came about.

Years and years before, it had come to the notice of Eochaidh, the then chief of the Clancys, that out there in the big world to the east was something called the Roman Empire, and the sailors (really pirates) who had brought back this news also brought the proof of it – a large bag full of gold coins with the heads of several emperors clearly to be seen on them. A careful examination of this money (no one in Corca Baiscinn, least of all chief Clancy, knew what money was) created only a mystery.

'Could they be decorations, d'you think?' he asked his druid.

'Maybe,' murmured that wise one, peering at them suspiciously. 'But I'd be more inclined to think they're for some kind of a game', and he rolled one down along the table. Halfway down, it disappeared between the table boards and clinked on the floor.

'There you are!' he cried triumphantly. 'I knew right well that that's what they were for', and he strode out, smiling and nodding to himself, another great problem solved.

Clancy sat looking after him, a sullen expression on his face. 'With every year that passes, I'm getting sorrier I didn't make that fool finish the last three years o' his training,' Clancy said. 'Half of an education is the worst thing a man can have, d'ye know that!'

His guests all along the table nodded, smiled and made various agreeing noises, but no one took sides. That would be asking for serious trouble. To criticise a druid –

especially a half-druid – was dangerous, for such a man might know enough to bring evil consequences on you but not quite enough to take them away again. And to criticise your chieftain was to invite penury on yourself – and, worse, on your wife and children too. So men made the right noises and held their peace.

But Clancy was not one to leave well enough alone. That night in his chamber, while fingering those gold Roman coins for the twentieth time, he began to pay attention to the heads stamped on each of them. And whatever about the coins' use, there was something in the way those proud men (whoever they were) held their heads. There was nobility in it, confidence.

And the conclusion he came to was typical of the man: 'If they can do it, why can't I? Anyway, amn't I better-looking than any one of 'em?'

But there was one thing he could not decipher: the inscription on each coin, for from his misspent school-days he had only been a poor reader, ever.

So first thing the following morning he sent for the druid again.

'Read them for me,' he told the druid, holding out a fistful of coins.

And the druid did so, faltering over the unfamiliar words: 'Augustus . . . Imp. Rom.', then 'Titus. Imp.', followed by Claudius, Nero and several more.

'What do them words mean?' Clancy asked.

'Their names, as far as I can tell.'

'As far as you can tell!' shouted Clancy. 'Either you know or you don't know. Get out o' here an' don't let me see your face again until you have a definite answer for me.'

The druid scurried off, leaving Clancy growling to himself, 'Bloody eejit . . . drown him, only that . . . be trouble from Tara . . . ', and so on.

He was angry enough to follow the matter up, though, and the first thing he did was to summon once more the captain of the sailors who had brought the gold in the first place.

'Remind me again, where did you come on these . . . these bits o' gold an' silver?' he asked.

The captain, a veteran on many 'trading expeditions' to Britain and Gaul, feared no man, and he showed that now by making only the tiniest of bows in the presence of the chief.

Clancy noted this too, but decided to ignore it for the moment. He could always have the fellow knifed later in some *shebeen* or other. These sailor types were great drinkers, he knew, and Corca Baiscinn *poitín* (the chief export of the place), even in small quantities, left a man in only a poor condition to defend himself against armed enemies from behind.

'I'll do that, *tiarna* Clancy,' he laughed. 'But I better tell you first that there's a name for the same bits o' gold an' silver.'

'D'you mean it?'

'I do. Coins, they call 'em in the Empire o' Rome.'

'Coins, eh? An' what are they for? Is it to decorate women, by any chance?' The captain eyed him oddly, blinked, then scratched his head and nodded.

'I suppose you could, now that you mention it. But anywhere I ever went in the lands to the east I only ever heard o' the one use they had.'

12

'An' what was that?

Clancy was becoming impatient, though he knew by long practice how not to show it.

'Buying an' selling, o' course. Don't everyone know that! Once people see the emperor's face on the coin, they know 'tis real, an' anyone who refuses to take one of 'em insults the emperor himself.'

There followed a long conversation in which Eochaidh Clancy received several lessons in politics, economics and language never before heard or considered in Corca Baiscinn or in the kingdoms near it. He found out what an emperor was and how armies were paid in coins, not in cows, and he deduced for himself how much easier it would be to steal and hide coins than cows.

By the time the captain left him, he had put aside (for the moment, at least) all notions of assassination. Such a man, used properly, might be as useful as any druid . . . and come to think of it, *more* useful than one druid in particular! The employment of knife-men might still be a useful option. He smiled, then nodded. It had been a useful day's education: one he could see sense to, put into practice. If those not-very-good-looking men of Rome could do what they were doing, so could he.

And he did. For the remaining seventeen years of his rule in Corca Baiscinn, his people, like it or not, became accustomed to coinage, much of it made of timber (bog-deal, in the main), since metals of any kind were in short supply. And though their value was more often than not in dispute, the coins had at least one desired effect: they spread the likeness of Eochaidh Clancy to the four corners of his realm and among people who had never met him face to face.

Likeness, yes. But name, no. For in the dim recesses of Eochaidh's mind, a further notion was collecting itself: if these coin things were the makings of a huge empire like Rome's, maybe he should have a name like one of those lads on them.

He broached the notion to his wife, Fininne, casually after supper one evening. 'Would you have any objection if I was called . . . amm . . . Claudius instead of Eochaidh?' he asked.

She almost smiled, but knew him well enough to realise that this was no idle question. She smiled softly. 'Claudius Clancy. That sounds nice. Where did you get that notion?

'Oh . . . nowhere. Something that came to me in a dream, that's all.'

Dreams were his catch-all excuse, she knew, when something yet unexplainable was in the offing, so she held her peace and waited for more to reveal itself.

This time the *reacaire* as well as the druid was consulted. He was ordered to procure a number of sweet-sounding names of Rome that might suit the dignity of his noble lord, and he returned a week later with a list half as long as himself. In the presence of Clancy and all his retinue, he began to recite the names there in the hall of Dún Mór, the chief family dwelling, while a black gale from the Atlantic howled outside.

'Antonius . . . Beelzebub – '

'Hi! Hold on there,' shouted the druid. 'That isn't a Roman name. That's the name o' some kind o' devil or evil spirit.'

'Yerra, be quiet, will you,' snapped Clancy. 'Better be a devil than nothing at all.'

He motioned to the man with the list. 'Read on.'

And he did.

'Claudius . . . Domitian . . . Eusebius . . . Gaius' – and on down through the alphabet – 'Suetonius . . . Titus . . . '

'Hmmm! I like that one. But keep going.'

'Vespasian . . . Zenobius.' He looked up then into the quietness. 'That's it, your honour. All I could find.'

'Good, good. You have done well', and Eochaidh pulled a gold ring from his finger, tossed it to him.

'Th-thank you kindly, Lord Clancy.' And he bowed himself out, smiling.

But he had scarcely pulled the door shut behind him when Clancy shooed the others away, then called the captain of his guards to him.

'You know what to do,' he whispered. 'Make sure he has an accident. The same kind as the last man I gave that ring to. An' bring it back here to me safe. But don't kill him.'

The captain smiled, an evil grin. He needed to be told no more. He had not been promoted for nothing. There were seven notches on the hilt of his dagger, one for each of the fingers he had already amputated while reclaiming his master's ring. It was a task he relished. It made him feel important to know that no less a man than Lord Eochaidh Clancy trusted him with such private, delicate work.

From that time on, with Eochaidh's change of name to Claudius, this taking of Roman names among the Clancy lords of Corca Baiscinn had taken root, guided in each case by the deliberate touch of druid and *reacaire* alike (though usually with some misgivings on the druid's part). And in the following generations, that land was ruled, after Claudius, by Caligula Clancy, Brutus Clancy, Elagabalus Clancy and his two sons, Viciosus and Insanus – to the great indignation and scandal of all the tribes round about.

'Trying to get above themselves, they are,' was the general snarled opinion.

'A sure sign of ignorance. Isn't it plain to see they haven't one brain between the whole lot of 'em.'

And on it went, everyone with his own opinion, and no one afraid to express it anywhere – except, of course, in true Irish fashion, to the Clancys, face to face.

And to these, when no one seemed to be objecting to their abandoning of the old Gaelic ways, a further advance seemed advisable: why not declare Corca Baiscinn an empire? What was the point in having an emperor's name if what you ruled was not known as such?

And so, in April of the fourth year of the reign of Brutus Clancy, it was proclaimed at every crossroads: 'From next Tuesday on, ye're all living in the Empire of Corca Baiscinn. Rejoice, celebrate an' give thanks!'

The people were perplexed, of course, but paid no great heed. They were well used to the lunacies of their rulers. The best thing to do, they knew, was to shout agreement, look enthusiastic, then go about their business as usual. Nothing would change for them. That was the one certainty that living in this part of the world had taught them.

But now, thirty-seven years to the day from the proclamation of the empire, Boethius Clancy, the current holder of the imperial throne (which, incidentally, was constructed from Moher flagstones, held together with dowels of blackthorn) was in no little difficulty. For he was a man with ambitions, this Boethius, one of them being to make good the sentence croaked by his mother just after he was born: 'He feels like a child that could rule the world some day.'

After those words, she promptly departed on *slí na fírinne,* and the boy was brought up by a series of nurses who never allowed him to forget what his mother had said, and by a father whose great love of *poitín* left him in no condition for anything else.

Long before his father's death, the young man could see clearly enough what that parent's neglect was doing to Corca Baiscinn: what few roads it had had were now noted more for weeds than travellers, the rushes seemed to be growing higher every year, and even the stones in the fields appeared to be swelling and spreading.

The young man's name was Bothlam. He had been named thus only because his father was too drunk to object on the day it was done by two of the nurses, women of a traditional mindset from near Loop Head who saw their opportunity to draw the Clancys back out of the mire of foreign names they had been sucked into. The child had been taken to the nearest river, doused in the cold water by one of them, then lifted out by the ears by the other and held up, and his new name, 'Bothlam', had been shouted at him three times. That made any changing of it nigh-on impossible. Permission would have to come from the chief druid of all Ireland (and he was noted as a man unfriendly to experimentation in such matters).

Bothlam began to show a hatred of the past, and who could blame him? It had swept away his mother and made his father into what he was now. And since Corca Baiscinn in the present was not a pleasant place, he drew a conclusion that had at least some sense to it: the future was what mattered, not the past. And he would control that same future, come what might.

And the very day his father died, he began. His name he changed at once from Bothlam to its nearest Roman equivalent, Boethius, and let the druids think what they liked.

'Ahhh!' he sighed immediately after the change of names, 'that feels a lot more comfortable on me.' And when his three royal brothers disagreed, it was noted with fear and wonder how they all, for some strange reason, jumped together off the cliffs of Moher one rainy morning less than a week later. 'The dark weather, surely, that made 'em do it' was as near as anyone ever came to solving the mystery. But after that, there was no more talk about the matter. Boethius was their lord's name now. That was that.

And Boethius, looking into the future, began to see salvation in grass. Where there was grass, there could be sheep, sheep meant wool, and wool meant gold and silver – for real coins, instead of the timber ones which no one outside of Corca Baiscinn would accept as anything but a joke.

He ordered that fields, especially rocky ones, were to be levelled and reclaimed, and when the workers complained that many of the stones were special – dolmens, *galláns* and such – and should not be interfered with, he ordered his foremen to weed out such troublemakers immediately.

'Twenty lashes for talk the like o' that,' he ordered. 'Sure, isn't a stone a stone, no matter what way 'tis standing. Oul' *ráiméis* an' stories like that are the ruination o' this land.'

And so, one by one, the ancient monuments left by the Firbolgs, the Tuatha Dé Danann and other vanished races were either dug up or pulled down all over Corca Baiscinn, much to Boethius's satisfaction.

'Now we're going somewhere at last,' he said, delighted, to Fraoch, his druid, one day in early autumn as he inspected yet another demolition site, this time of a large dolmen at Leacht na nUasal. 'When them rocks are broke up, they'll put a fine skin on another bit o' road,' he commented to his druid.

The druid smiled a frozen little smile but did not reply. He was becoming more and more frightened by his master's destruction of all things old in his lands. He should be voicing protest, he knew, no matter how violently Clancy might react. But that was easier said than done. Boethius, in one of his mad fits, was no respecter of persons, and even a druid's grey cloak might provide only poor protection against him.

Yet if this vandalism went on, word of it would sooner or later come to Tara. And then, the consequences would probably be far worse. It was an unenviable problem he had on hand – but one that was about to be settled in a way that no one wanted, but which should have been expected.

It was the following year, on May Eve – a day on which sensible people stayed at home if at all possible. Whatever work had to be done on that day could wait until the next, for it was well known that the Good People were given to moving their residences then, and woe betide the person who met them on their travels. Terrible injury or worse was to be expected from such a meeting, so no chances were taken.

Except in Corca Baiscinn, that is. For Boethius Clancy, a short time before, had revealed his newest strategy. 'If I'm going to conquer the world,' he had announced to all those he had invited to his feasting-hall, 'a good straight road out o' this *dún* is the first thing I'll need.'

Minutes later, he stood at the main gate and looked out at the narrow, meandering path that had served his ancestors so well, then declared: 'That'll have to be widened. How could any army look either dignified or frightening stumbling from side to side on a *boreen* like that?'

It was a question not easily dismissed, and so work had begun almost at once. Smooth and rapid progress was made for the first half-mile, until they reached the stream which flowed at the foot of the hill on which the fort was built. Here it was that their problems began. Quite innocently, too. The foreman in charge that day was a precise man, from Turoe in Galway, one who understood stone and was proud of the fact that he had completed jobs in many parts of Ireland for dozens of chiefs with never a complaint. He surveyed the fine flagstone carrying the bridge over the stream. It had been well laid, whoever had been responsible. A pity to have to move it.

He decided to seek Lord Clancy's advice.

'*A thiarna,*' he said, bowing, when they stood together on the bridge. 'This stone is as old as the world – '

It was the wrong approach. Clancy, as soon as he heard that hated word 'old', spat out at once what was in his mind. 'All the more reason to shift it out o' the way. What I want here is a timber bridge, one that'll give loud notice to our enemies that we're marching out, an' a warning to us any time we're being attacked.'

'But . . . but . . . '

'See to it! This very hour!' were Clancy's final words on the matter as he strode off, leaving the foreman with no option but to order the destruction of one of the most solid little structures his practised eye had come across in many a long day. But though he knew Clancy meant the stone to be broken up for road-surfacing, his pride in his trade would not allow him to give the order to do it.

The ten men who were detailed to move it asked him several times: 'Why can't we just smash it?'

'Because I'm telling ye not to. An' be careful down there. Don't damage it with that crowbar, you *gamall.*'

They snarled, but obeyed.

Under his eagle eye, they raised it, slowly, slowly, heeled it up on its edge and let it flop back, downside up, on the river bank nearest the *dún.*

It was then, unknown to anyone, that the sky, or at least the first fragments of it, began to fall on the Clancys and on the empire of Corca Baiscinn.

The foreman was the first to notice the shine, then the footprints. Even the oafish, growling labourers paused. They knew, even if they could not fathom it, that they were looking at something not ordinary. For there before them, on the underside of the bridge flagstone, were the delicate prints of seven feet, in a circle, and the surrounding surface of the stone was shining as though it had been polished that very hour. It gleamed in the morning's weak sunlight, and not because of any wetness. No, it was totally dry, yet shining.

No word was spoken as each one of them tried to fit the lore he knew to this strange thing.

It was the foreman's voice that shook them back to reality. 'Get the druid, one o' ye! Quick!'

When Fraoch arrived – at a trot, too – one glance was enough to tell him that something had been done that should not have been done. He ignored everyone there, as though they did not exist, made straight for the flagstone and fingered it, his eyes closed all the while.

'Oh! Oh! Oh!' he sighed, the sigh becoming a moan as he knelt there, his head falling forward. 'How can this day's work ever be undone?'

He blinked, licked his lips and looked about nervously. Those watching him at that moment felt anything but confident. Lips twitched. Tongues licked. Fingers scratched aimlessly. Was the world at last about to end, as had been so long promised? Was the Dark finally in its hour of triumph? Or was it merely that the Men in Black, those vampires from the godless East, the court of Tara, were now to have free reign to plunder the people of Corca Baiscinn? The options in the minds of those bystanders as they watched were all dark, all terrifying.

But when Clancy arrived back – as he was bound to, since work had stopped completely – it was at a saunter, looking about him as if at a *féile* gathering, his manner genial.

'Well, well, men! I'm told there's a bit of bother here, eh.' He looked at the flagstone. Then at Fraoch. Then at the foreman. But in his eyes there was mortal danger, and they saw it. His stare said, without words, though more clearly than any words could have conveyed it: 'If this bridge isn't finished – an' soon – heads will roll!'

No one moved. Then, for the first time in his young life, Fraoch stood forward, and spoke without fear. Whatever the consequences, he had had enough. What he had seen this morning had convinced him that *this* stone, whatever about all those others, should not be further desecrated. It could lead only to ill.

'Boethius Clancy' – even his mode of address was formal now, worthy of a druid – 'what you ask here is wrong,' Fraoch began. 'Wrong! And misfortune will be its end. Leave this madness! This stone – look closely at it! – was placed here to protect your people's *dún* from evil powers, though none of us realised that until today. Has it not done so? Are we here, or are we not, to talk about it? Be satisfied with what you have, in the name of Lugh, of Breas, of Danu . . . '

He was still invoking each and every god that was familiar to them all when Boethius cut in sharply. 'Silence! Cease this gibbering! When I order something to be done, I *expect* it to be done. An' I'm saying again now what I said before – though ye don't seem to listen too good! – if this bridge isn't finished this very day, there'll be widows wailing tonight.'

Another chief might have flounced off, content to threaten to get his will obeyed. Not Boethius Clancy. He looked about, then focused on the foreman. 'Here, you! That hammer.'

He beckoned impatiently to where a large sledgehammer lay by the side of the path. It was, with a bow, placed in his grasp.

"'Tis a poor thing that I have to show ye myself how a job like this should be done, but if men today are grown so stupid, then let it be so.'

He said no more, only clomped onto the flagstone with his hobnailed sandals and swung the hammer up and back, as though he were wielding his great sword in battle.

The druid leaped forward, hands up, and screeched: 'Don't! I know something else too. This *leacht* was where the Tuatha Dé Danann used to hold their dances. Look at the shine on it, the print of their feet. Do you want to bring their anger down on top of us for evermore?'

As soon as he said this, every eye there was nailed on Clancy. What would be his reaction? Anyone who had ever even spoken ill of the Tuatha Dé Danann, never mind interfered with their property, had come to an awful end. If Boethius Clancy desecrated this sacred place of theirs, what would befall his subjects?

Several shouts went up, and snarls of anger the likes of which no Clancy chief had ever before faced from his own men. But this seemed to make him only more determined. 'Keep out o' my way,' he growled at the druid, then thrust him roughly aside and aimed again.

This time there was no mistake. Up swung the hammer, back, then it whistled down on the stone. There was a sound as of splintering glass as hammer and stone met, then a crack crept from one side of the stone to the other and it broke into two perfect halves. Clancy leaped back as they collapsed into the stream, but in those seconds before they struck the water a cloud of white smoke billowed out from between them, out, out and up, in the shape of a – could . . . could it be!? – a huge salmon. Before all those frightened faces, it held its shape for a moment, then gradually faded.

There was silence for several seconds, then Fraoch whispered, fear in his voice, 'Something was let out here today. Ye all saw it. And I fear someone will suffer because of it.' He did not look at Clancy as he said it, but everyone there knew who he was referring to.

The only one who seemed to be unworried by all this was Clancy himself. He cleared his throat loudly and spat into the stream. 'Hah! That's what I think of all them oul' nonsense stories. Fit for frightening children only. A small bit o' morning fog up out o' the water an' ye're all shaking like leaves. 'Tis enough to disgust any real man.'

He snorted, leaving them in no doubt what he thought of them, then turned to go – but not without a finger of warning to the mason.

'Start this new bridge today. Or there'll be crying this night!'

He clomped off, muttering, shaking his head at the stupidity of those it was his heavy and thankless duty to rule.

Nor did it seem to trouble him any further in the days that followed. That his bidding was being done and the road rushed ahead (under a politic mix of threats and kindness) was enough for him.

Each morning he came to the gate of the *dún,* looked out at the previous day's progress and observed with satisfaction the straight, wide highway that was creeping further and further.

'Ahhh!' he sighed then. 'The day is nearly on us when I'll be leading the men o' Corca Baiscinn down an' out there to conquer the world an' fulfil my mother's prophecy.' (Her words had now become no less than this – a prophecy – in his mind.)

He was right in one respect: the day was coming when he would lead his men down the new road and across the elegant wooden bridge. But in a manner far, far different from what he imagined.

Not long afterwards – well within the year and a day that the old people gave as the time that retribution for especially evil deeds might overtake the doer – Clancy was enjoying himself hugely. It was a Friday night and the *dún* sparkled with candle- and lamp-light. A feast was in full, roaring swing in celebration of . . . of . . . ? No one could remember too clearly now, since much *poitín* had been drunk (each guest had brought at least the two customary flagons). But the feeding was still going on apace, a constant procession of servants shouldering heavy platters from the kitchen to the crowded hall.

Roars of jollity mixed with hisses of amazement as each new dish was uncovered, all this mingled with the thud of bodies on stone as this or that man slid under the table or collapsed from the weight of drink, and was either licked or chewed by the enormous wolfhounds that constantly padded restlessly about. And all the while, Boethius sat smiling at the proceedings.

Then the double doors swung open again. But this time there was a difference. Two trumpeters stepped smartly forward, blasted the heavy air with a barrage of sound, then moved slowly up the hall, still playing. They were followed by four servants carrying a huge silver tray on which rested Clancy's favourite food – salmon. This was no ordinary fish, though. For one thing, it was huge: at least forty pounds in weight, and more than five feet in length. At a regal pace, the procession made its way up the hall, two more servants bringing up the rear, each carrying sharp implements for the carving of this royal dish.

They stopped before Clancy's place and bowed. Then the chief steward arose. He looked severely about him, to all sides of the hall, and gradually men grew quiet. Even the dogs peering out from under the tables paused to listen.

'Take note, men of Corca Baiscinn,' the chief steward said. 'A meal fit for an emperor, for the conqueror of the world', and he pointed at the steaming salmon in its dish, then beckoned a little man to the table. He hurried forward, pulled a dagger from his belt and paused. Clancy rose and jabbed a finger towards a particular part of the salmon.

'There!' he ordered, and the small man plunged the dagger into the fish, cut a neat square from its flesh and raised it on the knife-point. Then, facing the feasters, in full view of all of them, he ate it. There was a hush as he swallowed it, then stood there, licking his lips.

After several moments, he nodded towards his master. ''Tis fine, your highness. No poison there.'

The whole hall seemed to sigh, as even those befuddled by drink let out a breath of relief. Now the *real* eating and drinking could begin in earnest. What had gone before was a preparation only, a light snack to untighten stomachs for serious feasting. It would be a banquet to remember, this one. Everyone was sure of that. Tonight, Corca Baiscinn. Tomorrow, the world! Yee-hoo!

But for some reason, that night Clancy did not sit erect, silent, as was his usual custom, and wait for his carvers to portion out the royal salmon, as they knew so well how to do. No. Something, of a sudden, urged him to rise and carve his own portion, even as those whose task it was stood there, in mid-motion, puzzled. But they knew better than to interfere and so stood back, thinking that maybe *poitín* was having its say, or that the forthcoming conquest of the world had made him forgetful of ordinary habits for the moment.

In any case, he did the job – messily, too, they noted – then sat back while two other servants loaded his plate with all else that was necessary. How could they have known that this little aberration, this hiccup in the feast, was anything but an accident?

Yet someone should surely have suspected that something was amiss when, three days before this feast, all the salmon in the large stone holding-pond behind the fort had disappeared overnight. This was where all fish were normally placed alive when the net-men delivered them prior to each celebration, since Clancy was particular in the extreme. 'A salmon that's dead more than three hours before I eat him isn't a salmon at all,' he was fond of saying. 'I might as well be eating timber. An' I never like eating timber.' There had been annoyance, of course, even anger, at the daring theft, but swift orders were issued to the net-men to bring replacements, and quickly.

They tried, in all their usual well-fished pools, but not a single salmon could they find. They were mystified. Never before had such a thing happened. They said as much to the steward, only to be warned harshly that their lives were at stake if they did not bring him a very different answer – and soon!

The same man was in his chamber, trying desperately to pick words that might, at least danger to himself, explain to his master how matters stood, when a loud rapping was heard at the rear gate.

One of the guards peered down from the catwalk. 'Well? Who are you? What d'you want?'

'Who is in charge of the kitchen here?'

The guard paused and looked more closely at the man below. The figure was very tall, and thin, his head – all of him, in fact – swathed in a black cloak. 'Who – who are you?' the guard asked.

The stranger merely half-smiled, stared at him, and said quietly, 'Who I am is not of importance. Only bring the main kitchen-man here to me. At once! Or this day's light is the last your eyes will look on.'

The even, knowing way he said it, with no threat, yet with something far more sinister, frightened the guard. He squinted again at the dark one, then scuttled off to the steward's door. A few words, and that man was hurrying to the back gate.

He clambered up the ladder and looked down. 'Yes? I'm the man you asked for. What d'you want with me?'

The one below seemed to snigger. 'Me? Want? Maybe you are the one who wants. They tell us that the chief of Corca Baiscinn – '

'– the *emperor* of Corca Baiscinn, to you,' growled the steward.

A pause. The stranger's gaze crept up along the wall, finally fixed itself on the steward's, held his eye. He smiled. 'Emperor?! Well . . . maybe. Howsoever, it has come to our notice that there are no salmon for his great feast. Is that true, or not?'

The steward peered down again. The man below was unstirring.

'Yes. 'Tis true. Why? An' who's this "us" you keep talking about?'

'That is not your concern. But the other matter, your salmon problem . . . Maybe that can be solved.'

The steward was, of a sudden, all ears. For well he knew that he was first in line for blame if Clancy's favourite dish was not before him at the appointed moment. With that thought uppermost, it never occurred to him to ask how the stranger knew of their predicament. He nodded to the guard, the gate was opened and they surveyed their visitor – or, rather, he surveyed them.

'Well?' said the steward. 'What can you do for us?

'This.'

The black cloak was swept aside, and there in his left hand, held by the tail, was the finest salmon the steward had ever seen – and he had seen many.

The fish weighed forty pounds, if not more, his practised eye told him, yet the tall man held it as though it were a wisp of straw.

This was no time for such observations, though. Here was salvation. The gods were indeed looking down on them.

Later, when asked where he had caught such a magnificent fish, his reply was vague: 'Oh . . . down there below the bridge', but in the flurry of preparations for 'the Feast of the World', as it was being called, no one pursued the matter further. The celebration could now go ahead as planned. That was good enough for them.

And the feast *had* gone ahead. The man in black had been paid in gold, had been invited to stay for the big occasion but had declined pleasantly and bowed himself out. Now here they were, everything running smoothly, everyone in a state of excellent cheer.

Clancy's plate was full and overflowing now and the servers had moved on up and down the table, heaping other plates just as high, a chunk of salmon taking pride of place on each. And the smell of that same salmon: Ahhh! Clancy's thumb flicked over and back across his knife-edge, impatient to get started. But etiquette held him back a minute or two longer, until all at the top table had been served. The soon-to-be Emperor of the World must, after all, show some kind of restraint. (At least he had been told so, though he did not yet clearly understand why. 'Hmm, I must ask Fraoch about that some time' was his last conscious thought before raising his knife-hand.)

Then 'Fall at it, men!' he bellowed, and a hundred faces plunged down into a hundred platters. Clancy observed all this with pride. This was one aspect of tradition he had no argument with. It was a pleasure to see so many people enjoying their food – as simple as that. He watched, smiling, as those around him, noble and lowly alike, snorted and guzzled their way through their platefuls, surfacing for air occasionally or to chew or spit, then returning for another, and another, bout of wolfing.

Somewhere in the midst of this happy scene, Clancy began to partake, but in moderation. And then it was the salmon he was chiefly interested in. One after another, he hacked out three large portions of it, savoured each one, teeth watering, eyes closed.

And then it happened. As he swallowed that third delicious mouthful, a sharp pain sliced along his throat, downwards. Then stopped halfway.

'Khk-akh!' His back arched and his hands clasped his neck. 'Uh-khu-agh!'

Something was stuck there. He tottered to his feet, gasping, mouth gaping, his face turning blue now. But in all that merriment, the eating, the snorting, he was scarcely noticed.

Until he heeled backwards, that is, his eyes starting from his head, and crashed to the floor with a strangled croak.

There was a stunned pause, then a foolish silence of several moments while men gawped, swayed, blinked, still not fully aware of what was happening.

The druid was the first to realise that something was extremely wrong. He sprang to his feet, clambered to Clancy's side, rolled him over and began to thump his back. It improved things not at all.

His master was breathing frantically now in short gasps, scrabbling at his neck, his mouth wide open, his face navy blue. Only the whites of his eyes were visible, the pupils rolled backwards and up. He looked a frightful, frightening sight.

'Do something!' roared the captain of Clancy's body-guard, shaking the druid violently. 'Don't stand there looking at him!'

Fraoch, who looked now as though something had just at that moment dawned on him, clapped his hand to his mouth, turned and sped from the hall.

'Where's he going?' snarled the captain.

'Never mind that. Stick your hand down the master's throat, quick, or he's a dead man!' shouted another.

'Me? Why me?'

But as they argued pointlessly, a new sound arose from their emperor – a harsh, rasping gurgle. There was immediate silence as they looked at each other, terrified now. Each one of them had heard it before as they knelt by dying friend or foe on this or that battlefield. Boethius Clancy was in his death throes. Not one of them could deny it. And it filled them with fear. This was the Feast of the World, for the Emperor of the World. And here he was, choking to death!

'Hell's curse on that eejit Fraoch! Where is he at all?' the captain bellowed.

At that very moment, the man himself rushed in, his book of knowledge in his hand. But it was too late. Clancy was dead. Of that there could be no doubt at all.

Those who had been drunk sobered up quicker than they had ever done before. Those who had been close to him began to keen. Most of the others just stood in a stupefied silence, while the dogs, fearing bodily injury, crept into the deepest shadows and awaited the worst. Not for long were they to be disappointed.

After the first terrible shock, the news spread like flood

water, down the new road, out over the countryside: 'The Emperor is dead! Boethius Clancy is gone from us. What'll we do at all? We're doomed! Finished!'

And thus it was that the man who would rule the world, who hated the past, levelled fairy forts, tore up *leachts* and feared not to interfere even with the property of the Tuatha Dé Danann, the man who revelled in the nickname 'Carraig' – the rock – met his unheroic end by such an unheroic weapon as a fish bone.

When those shattered people, calmed a little by the exhortations of the druid – 'That man lying there would want us to be dignified in our grief, and in the name of the divine Lugh let us not disappoint him,' and more of the like – had at last reconciled themselves to the fact that the worst had indeed happened and that there would now be no Empire of the World, smaller but more practical details were able to present themselves. And the first of them was the wake and funeral. No expense must, or would, be spared in showing the people of all Ireland that a great hero, a noble warrior, a man of wisdom, generosity and honour had been lost to the world. (Whether Corca Baiscinn could afford such a show could be considered later.)

And the more they talked about it, the more they came to believe what they were saying. Which was why each of the forty-one runners that were sent out the following day was given strict orders to stop nowhere without proclaiming the terrible news: 'The Emperor of Corca Baiscinn is dead. The end o' the world is only a short distance away – an' just as well. 'Cos what good is life without that hero among all heroes, that man who was only one step below a god?'

There was always a pause, an intake of breath, when they said that, even among listeners whose interest in such high matters was less than little.

'Whoever gave 'em that message must have a powerful load o' *poitín* drank,' was the general opinion whenever they proclaimed it.

Still, the runners did their duty, right or wrong, and the message *did* spread quickly to the five corners of Ireland: to Eamhain Macha, Teamhair Luachra, Lios na gCearrbhach, Ráth Croghan, Dún Ailinne and other important places. But, Tara, naturally, was where it came to first.

Unfortunately, things were not as they might have been at the court of King Cormac just then. For one thing, he was not himself – and that because he had a dose of something that had laid him low, had confined him to his room for a week already. And King Cormac, when he was ill, was not a man to be spoken to, never mind trifled with. And so, when the news of Clancy's death came and was delivered to the royal bedchamber, the reaction was less than expected.

'Unnnnnggghh! Ghhhhk! Clancy? What's that? Huukkkhnngh!'

'Ahm . . . the emperor of Corca Baiscinn. He's dead, your highness. Yesterday.'

The messengers were breathless – and not from running only. There was fear too, for in these royal, unfamiliar surroundings might lurk all kinds of dangers. As was now proved. For mention of the word 'emperor' seemed to change everything. Suddenly Cormac heaved himself up on his pillows, scattering the attendants who were dabbing cool water onto his face with soft cloths.

'Emperor? What emperor? There's only one emperor in this land, an' that's me – even though I never used the title yet. I wouldn't degrade myself by trying to copy what they call themselves in the Eastern World.'

He found strength to spit as he said this final word, and there, efficient as always, was a Servant of the Bedchamber to lick it up eagerly, instantly. (And that wonderful moment would pass down the generations: 'Our family are the guardians of the Royal Spit. That's a relic of the noble past – of the times when there was honour, loyalty and friendship in the land of Ireland.')

As soon as the lowly one had saluted and stepped back smartly, Cormac manhandled himself out onto the floor, groaning. 'Tell me again what you told me just now,' he snarled. And they did, fearing for their lives.

But they need not have worried. Cormac had never yet sunk as low as executing the bringers of even unwelcome tidings, and he had no intention of doing so now.

'The word is out, Your Highness, to every king in Ireland, an' you're the first to hear it, apart from the close neighbours at home,' one of his servants told him.

Cormac knew well what this betokened: an invitation to the wake and funeral. And that meant three days and at least three nights of solid drinking while the ceremonies were in progress. A man would need the constitution of a brace of horses to survive even one such occasion every five years. And, in his present condition, that one alone might do Clancy more damage than he was worth.

Yet . . . yet . . . wake-houses were useful places to meet other men of authority. At wakes, many feuds had been mended, plots hatched, debts collected, treaties signed (also broken), while men were yet in a serious frame of mind.

Sitting there on his gold-plated bed-edge, he considered further. But then he shook his head weakly, tumbled back onto the pillows and let out a groan. His happy interlude had passed. No! Corca Baiscinn's *poitín* he knew all about at first-hand. Oh, that party last Samhain! No, he could not risk it. Or he might be joining Clancy in the Other World. That he could do without just yet. Ireland needed him too much.

This thought lifted his spirits a little. So he called Fionn Mac Cumhail.

'Fionn, Boethius Clancy is dead,' Cormac told him, 'an' some one of us must put in an appearance. An' since I'm done up, it'll have to be you.'

'I'd be delighted, your Highness . . . Oh, sorry! I . . . I mean, 'tis no joy to me to be replacing you on such an occasion. But duty has to be done, an' I'll do it . . . with a heavy heart.'

'Good, good.'

'Can I take a few o' the Fianna, just to make it that bit important-looking?'

'Do what you like,' Cormac replied, and with another groan he turned to the wall. 'An' don't let me hear no more about Clancy or that bog-hole he called an empire until you come back.'

Fionn bowed himself out, smiling.

'Jealousy,' he thought. 'Isn't it an ugly thing that no

man, even the High King, can escape it?'

The king's final words were thrown after Fionn, as an afterthought: 'An' while you're at it, go down an' ask Taoscán Mac Liath has he my new medicine made up yet. That last stuff he gave me only made me worse. Boiled dung, it tasted like. Aa-nngghh!' And he clutched his stomach, very obviously in pain.

Fionn, as he strode across the courtyard, then down the hill to Taoscán's cave, was musing to himself: 'I'd rather be facing Croagh Dubh on a rainy night than going down to that cursed wake.' He was still thinking such thoughts as he knocked at the cave door.

There was no immediate reply.

'Anyone at home?' he almost sang, as he pushed it open.

He stopped suddenly, for there, hunched at the table, was his old friend Taoscán, but sitting across from him was a man he had never set eyes on before.

'Oh, I . . . I'm sorry, Taoscán,' he began, embarrassed. 'I didn't know you had a visitor.'

Fionn bowed slightly to the stranger, and then for the first time noticed his grey cloak. A druid! He was doubly embarrassed. He had, he was certain, in his blundering way interrupted these learned men in their discussion of some deep, knotty problem of philosophy or magic. But if so, the two men did not show it.

'Ah, Fionn! The very man we were talking about,' Taoscán said to his friend.

'Me? Why me?'

'That can wait. First things first. You're going to this wake an' funeral, aren't you?'

Fionn blinked. How could Taoscán know something he had himself found out only minutes ago? But he had no further time to wonder, for Taoscán was introducing him to the other druid.

'Meet my friend Theosofix. From Gaul, he is, on a visit to see how we manage our affairs over here. A man of learning and wisdom among his people, I can tell you.'

The other smiled modestly and bowed, as did Fionn.

Taoscán was introducing again: 'This is Fionn Mac Cumhail, leader of the Fianna of Erin. A good friend in battle, but a very bad enemy – as so many know to their cost.'

It was Fionn's turn to feel sheepish, but he merely shrugged, then sat.

'Now, this wake,' Taoscán continued. 'Under normal circumstances, it would not interest me much. But this man Clancy appears to have brought misfortune on himself. Several messages I have received of late from Fraoch, his druid, to warn me of how he was going from bad to worse, destroying things that are better left untouched. It disturbs me now that I failed to heed him. He is young and I thought he might be better left to face his problems alone, for the sake of experience. I was wrong, it seems. That is why I will be accompanying you, Fionn.'

He looked then at his friend from Gaul. 'And maybe it might be a good opportunity for this man here to see how we bury our dead.'

A flicker of nervousness crossed Fionn's face. 'D'you think 'tis the right time or place, Taoscán?' he asked. 'Maybe . . . wouldn't he be better off if you took him away down the Boyne for a day, or to see Sliabh Bladhma.

There's supposed to be lovely snails an' plants an' things like that out there.'

Taoscán's fingers began to drum on the table. A bad sign. His eyebrows bristled and he looked at Fionn directly. 'We're going to Corca Baiscinn, with or without ye. Now' – and he rose – 'go on up and collect whoever you're taking with you. And if you'll take my advice, you'll bring at least a dozen. It could get rough down there in the west.'

Fionn nodded and hurried out, but as he went he heard Taoscán's final words, low but clear: 'An' if you don't hurry, we'll be there before you.'

And strange to say, that was how it happened. By the time Fionn had chosen those who would accompany him – and this was no small task, since every man of the Fianna wanted to be included and was prepared to argue his corner – both druids were gone.

'Wouldn't you think they'd have the manners to wait for us,' scowled Conán Maol Mac Mórna, being his usual surly self.

'Aach, just because they have the power o' flying an' we don't, they like to show us up,' nodded his brother Goll.

'Look here, men,' said Fionn peaceably, 'this kind o' talk won't get us one step nearer Corca Baiscinn. If Taoscán Mac Liath is gone ahead of us, 'tis to clear danger out of our path. Remember that, an' stop muttering.'

And with those stern words, he led the twenty he had chosen west and south from Tara, intent on one thing only: to get to Corca Baiscinn in time for the wake of Carraig Clancy.

They made good progress, too. By the end of that day, by hard marching, they were at the Shannon, at the southern end of Lough Derg. But though they were tired, Fionn gave them little time to show it.

'We'll cross here,' he said, and he pointed to where the great river narrowed. 'Follow me!' And with only a short run at it, he leaped across, landing safely on the other bank.

One after another, the rest joined him without accident. He addressed them then.

'Ye all know how big the wolves are in this part o' the country.'

They nodded.

'A bite from one o' them lads could leave a man without his head, so what we'll do is build a fort here to protect ourselves during the night.'

They groaned, but he led by example, tearing up huge scraws and clods of earth, piling them into a bank almost as high as himself.

'Come on!' snapped Goll. 'We can't let it be said that he did the whole thing himself, or we'll be shamed.'

They stacked their weapons into a heap and very soon, in spite of their tiredness, a huge circular rampart was taking shape. By the time darkness came, it was finished, and they stood back to survey it.

'A fine piece o' work, even if I say it myself,' Fionn smiled, wiping his hands. 'Now sleep, an' I'll keep watch.'

The others needed no more encouragement. In minutes, their snores were sawing the air, and even Fionn's eyelids drooped.

When he awoke, it was dawn and they were all still safe. He stretched, ran three times round the outside of the fort, then called the sleepers. 'Right, men! Out of it!

We must be on our way, or we'll miss the wake.'

Within minutes, they were all up, about and eating whatever came to hand from their travelling sacks. It was little, but enough.

'We'll make up for it when we get to Corca Baiscinn,' Conán joked, but they, each of them. knew he was wholly in earnest. Someone would pay for this light breakfast, that was sure.

In half an hour's time, they were on their way west again, leaving behind them their fine fort (which later became known as Béal Ború, which was used by Brian, High King of Ireland, centuries later and which still remains to mystify and fill with wonder the visitor of today. It need not!).

Refreshed and looking forward now to the serious occasion before them, their steady pace ate up the miles until they began to overtake crowds of people, all hurrying in the same direction, all dressed in their best clothes, many of them weeping.

'Where might ye all be going?' Fionn asked gently of a golden-haired girl who was chewing her knuckles nervously.

'Is it so you don't know?' She looked at him in wonder.

'Know what, girl?' he asked, pretending innocence. She stopped now, stared up at his face, mouth open.

'Where are you from at all, stranger? Don't everyone know that the Emperor of Corca Baiscinn is dead! We're going to his funeral, where else?'

Fionn nodded, and let her go her way. 'We're on the right road, anyway, men,' he said.

All they had to do after that was hunch their backs, shorten their strides and try as much as possible to look like normal people. But this was only partly successful. Those they met with still gaped, and stared at these huge men from Lugh-knows-where. But thankfully, no one ran away from them or refused to speak to them. Everyone plodding west that day had other things in mind – the main one being the respect due to their chief, their hero, their protector, Boethius Clancy.

When they arrived finally at Dún Mór, overlooking Farrihy Bay, they were in almost a jolly humour from the constant talk and chatter, but as soon as the fort came into sight, a hush spread over the travellers. Each person in that crowd knew what was expected: good manners, respect. Quietly, they lined up at the front gate, each one staring solemnly in front, then filed in, step by slow step, to where Boethius Clancy was laid out in all the magnificence his family owned – or had been able to borrow or steal.

A strange place it was, too, the death-chamber. At the head of the bier stood a semicircle of six wild, red-haired keeners (brought from Aran at great expense for the occasion), each one in the last throes of pain, sorrow and misery, it seemed.

'If crying could wake the dead, Clancy'd be on his feet again by now,' was Fionn's first observation as he entered. His second was the figure of Clancy's wife, sitting silent and expressionless at the foot of the bed, accepting the sympathy of each visitor as though she were somewhere else.

And 'Carraig' himself? Where was the glory, the pride, now? As Fionn stared at the pale face a moment, a desire to laugh **passed over him,** but was as quickly quashed. No matter **how foolish, ridiculous** a man's life, his dead body demanded **respect, even if,** as in this case, his neck was black, **ugly and swollen.**

Fionn **paid his condolences** to the glassy-eyed widow, paused **a few moments in** silence beside the corpse, then passed **the red-headed banshees,** and so went on out. He was joined **in the yard** moments later by the others, one by one.

Goll **shook his head, and** spoke for all of them: 'By Crom, if **I had to put up** with them noisy *cailleachs* for long, **I'd be laid out on** that bed myself – or else they would.'

There **was general, if silent,** agreement about that. Fionn was just **about to add a few** words more when, 'Hhssst!', their **attention was urgently** demanded by a servant twenty yards **away across the yard.** He was gesturing them to him **frantically.**

'Uh-oh!' **sighed Diarmaid.** 'Trouble, I know it.'

He was **right. But for the** wrong reasons. As they were soon to **find out.**

When **they heard what** he had to say, they learned that that servant **was merely** passing on a message: 'A friend o' yours **is waiting for you.** There.' And he pointed to an oaken **door to his left.** They eyed it. Was this some kind of joke? **Or worse again,** a trick?

Goll, **mainly from** lack of something to drink, hissed, 'Come on! **We'll show** 'em how to enjoy themselves,' fingering **his sword** as he said it.

'No!' **ordered Fionn.** 'No weapons. Not yet. First let me find out **what's behind** this door.' Three steps, and he grasped the latch, drove the door inward and stood there on the threshold, ready, alert.

He would have laughed at what met his eyes – except that he dared not. For there, heads suddenly snapped towards him, each staring at him, were his friend Taoscán, Theosofix, and a third, a druid also, but a stranger to him.

'Sorry!' he stammered, stepping back hastily. 'My mistake.'

Taoscán rose. 'Not at all, Fionn. Come in. You're welcome. We were waiting for ye all.'

Fionn breathed a sigh of relief. For the second time in two days, he had blundered in upon druids at work, and he felt like a little boy among men.

But not for long. Because Taoscán, in his usual understanding way, was making the extraordinary seem everyday: 'Men of the Fianna, just as well ye're here tonight. For believe me, without clear heads and sharp swords, I fear we' – he glanced at Clancy's druid and his Gallic friend – 'might have to do what would please none of us to do.'

Fionn blinked. He did not grasp at once what he was being volunteered for here. But since it was Taoscán who said it, there must be sense to it, so he nodded agreement. 'All right. But what's happening here? That's all we want to know.'

'Indeed that isn't all. What's this I'm hearing about clear heads?' It was Goll. He had pushed to the front, an angry look on his face. 'Are ye trying to tell me now that after all our hurry to get here, there won't even be a drop to wet our throats?'

Fionn was on the point of speaking angry words to him when Taoscán cut in. 'Every man will get his just deservings, Goll. Have no fear of that.' And he pointed to a corner of the room. Everyone peered. There in the shadows was a little barrel, immediately recognizable. 'You can take that with you for a start, Goll. It'll keep your tongue wet for a while.'

And as the greedy one leaped forward to obey, Taoscán turned to the others with a sigh they all too clearly understood. 'Our arrangements for tonight are as simple as this, Fionn. Us three, we have this room here to ourselves during the time this wake lasts. This is just as well, for prayers must be said, and it is not out there' – he jabbed a finger towards the door – 'that much praying will be done, I think. We will come out occasionally, as we are needed, but otherwise we prefer the quiet here inside.'

Fionn could find nothing to argue with in that, and so he and all the others who had squeezed into the room behind him bowed themselves out. Only when the door was closed did it occur to him to ask: 'How did they get here before us? That's the first thing I meant to ask Taoscán.'

'You should know by now not to be surprised by anything a druid does or says, Fionn.' Liagán said it.

'True, I s'pose,' Fionn murmered, 'but I'd still like to know what way they came.'

'It wasn't any road we'd be taking, anyway,' Diarmaid nodded, 'if they came by road at all.'

'It'd be a fine thing to have time to work that out now,' said Fionn, 'but we'd better go back to where the crowd is or they'll be saying we're getting above ourselves an' don't want to mix with 'em. So scatter out, talk nice an' don't get pulled into any arguments.'

That seemed sensible advice, so they turned towards where the crowd was, each one of them excited at the prospect of real Irish entertainment of the old type, about which their grandparents, with misty eyes, had told them in their crippled, declining years by the fireside: 'Them were the wakes! Ahhh! When men were animals an' women tried to tame 'em. There wasn't a person died that time but three or four more were killed at the wake. But sure, them good times are all gone. The people in the world now aren't people at all, only *pusacháin* an' *donáin.'*

What they expected and what they found was, miraculously, the very same! For even in the yard, the noise was already rising. And so it should, for there were heroes and warriors (not all of them men, either) present, singers and scribes, from almost every territory in Leath Mogha and Leath Choinn. A noble array it was, between small and tall, battle-scarred and skin-smooth, dark and fair. O'Briens and McCarthys were there, Kerrigans, Kierseys and O'Connors, as well as Flahertys, O'Sullivans, Doyles and as many more surnames as could be counted on the average person's fingers and toes three times over.

And not a one of them that did not recognize Fionn and his companions. For they had all met at one time or another, on one side or another of battles up and down the length of Ireland. There were *'Fáilte*'s, and much slapping of backs and poking of ribs as they renewed old acquaintance. Yes, it had every prospect of being a gathering to remember.

And still the mourners kept coming. By the time darkness fell, the *dún* was mobbed, and it fell to Fraoch to break the bad news that no one else could be allowed to enter, 'For fear people'd be suffocated.'

There was much angry growling among the latecomers, O'Neills and O'Donnells among them, who had flogged their horses four days and nights non-stop to be present. But Taoscán soon put things to rights. He called Fraoch to one side, whispered something to him, and minutes later it was announced at the main gate that ten barrels of choice old Corca Baiscinn *poitín* would shortly be sent out 'to keep the frost off those outside whose nobility an' religion brought 'em here to honour the dead.'

A cheer – 'Yee-haaa!' – went up. 'Generosity was always Clancy's second name,' someone said.

'You're right there. A religious man, like all his people before him,' said someone else, and others added more of the same.

'Hmmm!' mused Taoscán. 'Whether that was so or not, we'll have peace for a while now. But for a while only. Drink always talks its own language, sooner or later.'

Meanwhile, inside, in the hall where the conquest of the world had been planned (or at least talked about), one room away from where its would-be Emperor now lay stretched cold and dead, there was much conversation, especially round the fire. And the odd thing was that the same fire was in a corner of that spacious room, not in the centre of a wall or even in the middle of the floor, as in other houses. And why? Simply because Clancy was always an awkward and suspicious man.

A fireplace where people could sit to left and right of it, never mind in front, had, in his mind, to be wrong. It meant equality. And in Corca Baiscinn the only equal person was the Emperor. So his father's fireplace had to be ripped out and rebuilt in a corner, where only he might sit, in solitary dignity.

It made things awkward now, on this night of mourning, for those gathered in. But they made the best of a bad job, and talked on.

Naturally enough, most of the conversation at first concentrated on the virtues of the man who was dead, all the battles he had won, the heads he'd split, the warriors he'd taken prisoner, the cattle he had liberated to a better life in Corca Baiscinn and the huge rocks he had lifted and cast without bursting his trousers or belt.

But as soon as those self-same rocks were mentioned and mulled over, it was only natural that someone would ask the obvious question: 'How did he get the name "Carraig"?'

And strange as it might seem, there was only one man from Corca Baiscinn in the death-room at the moment of that fatal question. But he was Murcha McMahon, and no one was better qualified than he to answer, for the same man, like the druid, had watched Clancy grow more and more unpredictable and impious for some time past, but had feared to say it. He was only a poor fisherman, after all, with a young family to rear, and if chieftains were losing the run of themselves, that was no business of his. He told it now, though.

'There's a story behind that, men,' said he with a sigh, pushing his feet forward into the ashes, 'an' I'll tell it to ye now, only gimme room to do it.'

In spite of the huge crowd pressing in, almost sitting on each other's knees, space was made somehow, and he began. But not before he had spent several minutes clearing his throat, spitting green snots into the ashes and gripping and ungripping his fists (in the manner laid down) – all signs of a formal beginning of great things to come.

*

Was it worth it, Fionn asked himself an hour later, when the *seanchaí* had finished his tale? Had they learned anything worth knowing? Was all this mouthing about the Tuatha Dé Danann's *leacht* just the invention of the storyteller's imagination, or was there some truth in it?

It was as if McMahon had read their thoughts. 'I can tell by the look in yeer eyes that ye don't believe all I'm saying,' he said. 'But ye can. That *leacht* I'm talking about was below there where the bridge is now that ye marched in over.'

There was a hush as he looked Fionn straight in the eye. 'Why don't you ask that druid ye brought with ye from Tara?' McMahon asked. 'He has the gimp of a man that'd know about things like that.'

Fionn nodded. 'I'll do that, never fear.'

But then the *seanchaí* turned to the crowd, rose, and rubbed his hands vigorously. 'Well, well, aren't we getting very *gruama* entirely. What we need is a song or two to liven us up. Who'll sing a few verses?'

'Begobs, but you're right,' shouted one of the Kierseys, a family always noted for their singing. 'D'ye want me to give ye a bar or two?'

'Good man! Do! Go on!' croaked two dozen voices, amid glugging and *súlaching* in *poitín*-bowls.

'Have ye anything in mind, or will I give ye one o' my own?' Kiersey said.

''Tis your choice, when you volunteered,' smiled Fionn helpfully.

And so, after the usual shuffling and clearing of his throat, Kiersey began in a high voice, and sang them 'The Rann of the Yellow Chicken', a long, complicated account of a magical fowl with terrible antisocial ways which attacked and ate people and their livestock alive, soiled their clothing when they tried to intervene, and was finally only brought to account by an enchanted spider. In spite of the unlikeliness of the tale, Kiersey sang it with the skill of a true *reacaire* and was applauded loud and long when he ended.

Now that the silence had been broken, there was no further difficulty in getting performers to do their party pieces, and soon a full-scale *céilí* was in progress, music for the dancers being provided by a small orchestra of *pus*-musicians from Sliabh Luachra, the very home of non-instrumentalists.

Several times Fionn had to intervene as the floor was battered, the house shaken by the eager feet of those steppers-out. 'Ah, here, men! Have a bit o' respect, can't ye? There's a man dead in the next room. Give the keeners a chance, at least.'

That seemed to make the dancers only redouble their noise, until the door of the druid's room was flung open and there stood Fraoch, his face like thunder. 'Quiet!' he bellowed, and an immediate hush fell. 'We can't even hear ourselves praying in here. Have ye no religion or decency at all?'

But the effect of his giving out was spoiled somewhat by the sight of Theosofix peering out over his shoulder, smiling, stroking his chin in wonder. He was obviously amazed and amused by this strange death-custom of the Irish.

Both druids had hardly withdrawn into their room again when the *pus*-music began once more, but this time not as loud. A warning finger from Fionn saw to that.

But if the dancing was less noisy now, it was, if anything, rougher than before. And as every dancer knows only too well, where there are bystanders crowding in, there are toes to be trampled, eyes to be knocked out by swinging elbows, and teeth, ears and noses to be injured in the course of the merriment.

All those occasions of misunderstanding and ire were there that night aplenty, but it was something else entirely – something unexpected – that began the row.

Men, as well as women, wore their hair long in those days, and in every gathering of dancers a favourite trick was to grab a fistful of hair of a ponytail as its owner swung by, pull, and listen for the 'Aahh-iaa!' That, no matter how often it was repeated, was regarded as the height of fun, the peak of humour. And on this night it was no different, though all present were chieftains, some of them even men of breeding and notable families.

In the middle of a particularly noisy dance-figure, a hand snaked out from the crush of bystanders and yanked. The hair it pulled belonged to a grizzled old chief of the O'Quinns from near the Giant's Causeway in Antrim, a ruffian – among rough customers, too. And, horrors! The hair came off. All of it, leaving a bare, sweaty skull glistening in the lamplight. A wig!

The dance shuffled to a halt. The music faded nervously. O'Quinn's hands were already clapped to his head, but the damage had been done. His secret was out, and giggles began to bubble up amid the lookers-on.

O'Quinn was anything but amused. His face darkened, his left hand streaked to his dagger.

But 'No!' . . . Fionn was already there, O'Quinn's arm grasped in a grip of iron. 'No knife-work tonight. Not in the house of the dead.'

O'Quinn struggled – uselessly – to release himself. Words came to him then, though, and Fionn let him talk. Better that than bloodshed.

'The man that took ma hair, ah'll kill 'im, so ah wull.'

'O' course you will,' soothed Fionn. 'An' you'd be well entitled to. But wait till the morning, an' you can kill him then in the daylight, when you can see him better.' Fionn turned then, picked up the wig and handed it back. 'Put that on you, now, like a good man. Or you'll get a cold.'

He beckoned to a servant then, whispered him to bring O'Quinn a treble measure of *poitín* (a 'quietener', as it was known), then shouted 'Music there! Are ye dead or alive, musicians?' They began again, as did the dance, and for a while all was peace and good cheer once more.

But there was only a certain amount of dancing that could be borne, and when all the known steps had been gone through ten times over and the musicians were noticeably tiring, Goll, a poor dancer anyway, growled, 'Is there nothing else we could be doing to pass the time except the oul' foolery?'

At another time, Fionn would have rebuked him for

his ill manners, but the truth was that he himself had begun to wish for a change. So at the next pause in the dance, he stepped into the middle of the floor, clapped his hands and announced, without making it seem like an order: 'People, ye have shown great suppleness of limb, lightness of foot, as well as nobility of countenance these past hours on the floor, but the time has come for something new. For there are some among us tonight who do not excel at dance. An' they too must have their chance.'

He paused, gazed around him at the crowd, saw at its edges many who were so far gone in *poitín* that nothing more should make any difference to them that night. Yet he noted the non-dancers, too, and they were listening, interested.

'Now, in my travels to wakes in all parts o' this land of Ireland over the past thirty years, I have seen many strange customs. But none of 'em as strange as the one that met me at the wake of O'Falvey Mór na gCluas in Corca Dhuibhne the year o' the great frost.'

There was much nodding, especially among the older spectators.

'We remember it well!'

'The frost, maybe, but how many o' ye know the game they use down there in Ciarraí to kill time at the wake, once the chief is dead?'

A shaking of heads.

'Well, I'll tell ye. 'Tis called "Horsey-horsey". Now d'ye know?'

More shaking of heads, furrowed brows. Only one or two nods, obviously from Kerrymen. 'Tell us about it,' someone called out.

Even some of the *poitín*-addicts were beginning to try to focus their eyes, now that the infernal music and dance had ceased.

''Tis like this,' Fionn went on. 'Three people have to volunteer: one to be the stallion, one a cob, an' one a pony. An' once they're out on the floor, they have to do whatever they're ordered to. If they don't, they're shamed. An' I can tell you, some o' the things they were asked to do at O'Falvey's wake, it'd put the hair standing on your head. I saw men humiliated that night more than if they'd run away in the middle of a battle.'

Silence.

'So, I'd advise ye to think carefully before offering to be the horse in this game.'

Men shuffled their feet, pursed their lips, thinking. No one volunteered.

'Come on, come on!' growled Fionn, scorn in his voice. 'Am I looking at a gathering of warriors or babies?'

That did it. O'Quinn clumped out into the centre of the floor. 'Ah'm afeared o' no silly game, especially one from that bog-hole Ciarraí. Ah'll be the stallion.'

And he grinned, no doubt seeing this as a way of proving himself a stallion of a man, not the bald old leftover he had appeared to be a short while before.

'That's good,' smiled Fionn. 'Now, who'll be the cob?'

'Who else but me?' growled a butty little man with a distinct Kerry accent, elbowing his way roughly through the crowd. Men eyed him closely as he faced O'Quinn. Dark-jowled the Kerryman was, and half-shaved, as if his barbering was done with a flint knife. Almost as wide as he was tall, he looked every inch a strong, rough customer.

'So, old man, you think Ciarraí is a bog-hole, eh?' the Kerryman challenged O'Quinn.

His voice was a low, dangerous snarl. But Fionn was not about to let a fight break out now. He cut in. 'Aha! A man from Ciarraí itself. Who better to know the game than yourself!'

The Kerryman smiled evilly. He had something unpleasant to teach O'Quinn, that much was clear to those standing nearest to him.

'But we still need a pony. Out now, men! Who'll it be?' Fionn demanded.

Goll Mac Mórna's hand shot up. 'I'll do it. Never let it be said that the Fianna won't play their part as good as everyone else.'

Fionn eyed him. 'Are you sure you wouldn't rather let one o' the younger lads do it, Goll?'

'Why would I? A bit o' fun is the best medicine in a wake-house. 'Twas Taoscán Mac Liath himself told me that. So no more talk. We'll start.'

Fionn shrugged. 'I hope you won't end up regretting it,' was all he murmured.

Then, in a voice everyone could hear, he explained the rules to the three horses. 'Now, 'tis as simple as this, men. Whatever anyone in the audience tells ye to do, ye must do it. No questions, no refusals, only do it. D'ye understand?'

All three nodded.

'Very well. I'll start the game, so.'

He turned to O'Quinn. 'Right, stallion. Something easy first. Jump over the table there. But don't disturb a single piece o' crockery.'

O'Quinn did it, and in style, too, with a foot to spare. A roar of approval went up from the crowd.

'Good, good. Now a small bit harder.'

Fionn reached for a stool, placed it on the table, then set a goblet of wine on it, filled to the brim. 'Can you jump that one, though?'

O'Quinn snorted, whinnied – he was fully in the spirit of the game now – and galloped at the table. He buck-leaped over it, just clearing the lip of the goblet, and landed with a crash on the floor.

Another yell of delight from the lookers-on. 'Great horse! Mighty beast!' and so on.

'Very good,' Fionn nodded. 'Take a rest now, stallion. You might be needed again later.'

O'Quinn almost pranced back to his place, delighted that his honour had been restored.

Then it was the cob's turn. 'Are you ready?' Fionn asked.

The Kerryman only growled.

'I'll take that for a "Yes".'

Fionn did not care much for this fellow's attitude. Maybe he should be taught a little lesson. 'A jockey. We need a jockey,' he shouted. 'Who'll be the one?'

At least a dozen men pushed forward, all anxious for sport.

'One at a time,' Fionn cautioned. 'But stand near. Ye'll be needed.' He smiled as he said it, knowing what was to come. But no one noticed that the Kerryman was smiling too.

A hairy monster of a Mayoman leaped onto the Kerryman's back with a shout, a knobby stick in his hand. 'Hup, *capall,* or I'll use this on you!' he shouted.

The cob galloped around the hall, faster and faster, as the crowd yelled encouragement, louder and louder. Three circles he had done when Fionn called for a second jockey. A red-headed O'Kelly jumped forward, grasped the Mayoman round the neck and midriff, and on went the cob, a little slower, but only a little. More shouting and encouragement.

Three rounds later, and Fionn waved another of the waiting jockeys into action. Then a fourth. And a fifth. But when the sixth perched himself shakily, dangerously, on the fifth, the hall became very nearly silent. Every eye was on this tough Kerryman now, for though his knees were buckling under him and his load was almost the height of the rafters, he was still struggling on step after painful step, refusing to give up.

One by one, the watchers' eyes began to flicker towards Fionn. The same thought was in every mind:

'End it. Now! The man has done enough.'

And he did – but only after the cob had staggered six steps further, teeth clenched, eyes screwed tight closed.

'That's enough. Race over,' Fionn ordered. 'Get off now.'

And they did, each one full of admiration, clapping their tough horse on the back and shoulders as they dismounted. Every other hand in the hall was clapping too, for a storm of applause now burst forth, and there were shouts of approval as well as stamping of feet. A goblet of *poitín* was thrust into the cob's shaking hands, and this quickly restored him. He bowed to all sides and flopped down, to continued applause.

In the midst of all this, Fionn caught Goll's eye and shook his head. He was not smiling. This would be a hard act to follow.

But Goll did not appear to think so. For as soon as the applause had died away, he rose, a bright look on his usually dour face. 'That was as fine an effort as ever I saw,' he said, gesturing towards the Kerryman. 'After what we witnessed here tonight, at least one thing is clear: no chief should be without Kerrymen.' And as his listeners began to nod agreement, he added, ' – as heavy warhorses.'

Goll grinned. But Fionn did not. Nor did the man from Kerry. His head jerked up, and despite his weariness he would have reacted in a manner that might have ended the night unpeacefully had not Fionn risen and addressed Goll.

''Tisn't that at all, but this. You volunteered for the game, so come on out there in front of everyone an' do your piece.'

'An what's that?'

'I'll give you your own choice, just to prove you can do better than what we saw here already – if you can!'

Goll laughed scornfully. 'Can? I *will,* an' very easy, too.'

The small Kerryman was glowering at him with blood-shot eyes, his lips moving, though no words came. He seemed angered by such confidence.

'D'ye ever see a horse walking backwards?' asked Goll, swaggering to the middle of the hall.

'O' course we did. Wouldn't any fool of a horse do that. If that's all you have to show us . . . '

He waved them to silence. 'Ah yes, but did ye ever see a horse walking backwards . . . upside down?'

Even the Kerryman blinked at that.

'How could any horse walk upside down, you big ape?' leered one of the O'Looneys.

In three steps, Goll was on him, and with a single thump of his mighty fist sent him spinning into a corner. 'Don't insult me by telling me what can't be done,' he snarled. 'If it can't be done, I'm the very man that can do it.'

'All right, all right!' squeaked O'Looney, attempting to gather himself up. 'I wasn't arguing with you at all. Take it easy, can't you?'

Several of O'Looney's friends stepped forward threateningly, fingering their daggers. There would certainly have been trouble there and then only for Fionn.

'Calm down, people,' he said quietly. 'Remember the dead man next door,' and in the few seconds of pause he nodded to Goll. 'Do your piece. Now!'

Goll bowed mickingly to the audience. 'I'll need a man to be a horse-dealer,' he said, smiling at them.

At once, before anyone else could move or reply, the butty Kerryman was out on the floor. 'I'm the very man for you.' That evil smile was back on his face as he said it, and this time Goll noticed it.

'Are . . . are you sure you know how to play this game?'

'Heh! Never, never doubt that much. The game with the dealer in it? "Horsey-horsey" we calls it in Kerry, where 'twas invented. Remember that. There isn't a version of it that I haven't seen played – as you'll find out soon enough.' Again that evil grin.

Goll hesistated now. He had an uneasy feeling . . . But only for a moment. 'Don't mind that oul' nonsense. That's only for children. Backwards upside down first. That's what I'm doing, or – '

'Ah-ah!' the butty one cut in. 'I'm the dealer here now,

horse, an' I'll call the tricks – the right way. The way they're called in Kerry.' He smiled, revealing several black stumps, which made him seem even more sinister.

'No. 'Tis my choice, an' I – '

The Kerryman swung round, laughed outright to the crowd. 'He wants everyone else to play by rules, but he won't do it himself,' he sneered. 'Is that the way a man of honour behaves?'

'It is not!' roared the O'Looney faction, and Fionn noticed that there was no one – not one! – who intervened on Goll's side. His earlier hasty behaviour had made him no friends.

Then the Kerryman was addressing Fionn himself. He spoke formally. 'Let you be the judge, Fionn Mac Cumhail, leader of Fianna Éireann, whether I'm playing this game correctly or not. You're the one who saw it in Kerry. If I do anything wrong, you be the one to tell me stop.'

Fionn nodded, resigned. Every eye was on him.

Goll was on his own now, for better or worse. And Fionn feared that it was for worse. Or even worse!

'Right, Mac Mórna,' the Kerryman sniggered, 'rise your tail.'

Goll glared at him. 'That's not a real trick. Ask me something right.'

The Kerryman looked knowingly at the crowd, nodded significantly.

'Failed at the first fence. Very interesting.' And he tittered. But then the smile faded. He looked at Goll directly. 'All right, horse. Something easier for you, so, since you're a bit thick. Wag your ears.'

Goll tried but could not.

'So, a disobedient horse, eh?' He paused a moment to make sure all in the audience were watching closely. But he need have had no fears about that. 'Is there anything at all you can do, stupid animal?'

Goll, out of narrowed eyes, glared at him. 'If you're trying to make little o' me – '

'Silence, disobedient animal!' shouted the Kerryman, and like lightning the back of his hand connected with Goll's cheek with a crack as of a whip.

Goll yelled, lurched back, but recovered in seconds, lunging for his attacker. But the Kerryman neither moved nor spoke. It was the crowd that replied. And loudly. 'Spoilsport! Play the game, can't you. Or else sit down.'

Goll eyed them, furious. 'An' let him hit me? No man ever did that an' got away with it.' He stamped his foot.

'I did,' chuckled the dealer. 'An' I'm not finished at all yet. But maybe *you* are, little horse.' He was smiling openly now for all to see.

Goll sank back. He would not allow this Kerry *bodach* to shame him and the Fianna. 'Go on with the game,' he snarled.

The dealer bowed, grinned again. 'Certainly, horse. Show me your teeth.'

Goll bared his yellow fangs, as frighteningly as he could. But this display was greeted with – Thwakkk! – a stinging slap across the mouth. He leaped back again – 'Awwkgh!' – but was back in an instant, fingers clenched to tear out the dealer's windpipe. 'You dirty – !'

But he got no further. Fionn's arm shot out, blocked him like a rod of steel. 'No! None o' that! Play the game. He's within his rights.'

And as Goll ground his teeth and breathed hard, Fionn added, 'Remember, you're the one that said nothing was impossible to you. This is your chance to prove it.'

A slow clap from the crowd told Goll that here, now, he was on his own. It was a thought that sobered him a little. He relaxed. 'All right. Call again. Whatever trick you like.'

'Good horse. You're learning fast. We won't be long training you at all, maybe.' And there was that dangerous leer again. 'Down on your knees, now, like a good animal.'

Goll sank slowly to the floor, wondering what was next to come. He had only moments to wait. The Kerryman, who had padded around behind him, vaulted onto his back, clenched two rock-hard arms about his neck, dug his heels into his kidneys and yelled, 'Now, horse, round the house with you, an' double quick!' As he said it, the nails of his right hand dug into Goll's chin, while his left hand battered blows on the warrior's cheek and neck.

And Goll lurched, stumbled, tried to run, but the space was so crowded that he tripped, then fell. Yet he struggled up at once, determined. He would show this savage *bastún* from the wilds that the men of the Fianna were not to be mocked.

But the man on his back seemed to understand this only too well, for his heels gouged ever more deeply, his nails clawed more viciously, while all the while the crowd gurgled and whooped with delight. Rarely had any of them been so well entertained, at wedding, wake or victory feast.

At last Goll, in spite of his determination, stumbled to his knees, breathless, then fell forward in a heap under the dealer's weight.

'Lazy horse! You must be punished!' the Kerryman

shouted. He sprang from Goll's back to the fireplace, snatched up a heavy, knobbly cudgel from the pile of firewood on the left-hand side, grabbed one of his horse's "hooves" and began to hammer and batter mercilessly at the sole while the crowd gawped and Goll yelled blue murder. Then the other foot got the same treatment, and though Goll used every ounce of his huge strength to try to get away, the man from Kerry held him in an unbreakable grip and never relaxed it until he had finished. By then, Goll could barely stand, the soles of his feet a bruised and throbbing mess.

During all of this, Fionn stood by, silent, and when Goll at last groaned for help, the answer he got was not encouraging: 'You're the one who volunteered for this game. You'll have to finish it out alone, I'm afraid.'

But just then, for no known reason, all passion seemed to leave the Kerryman at once. As if nothing at all out of the ordinary had occurred, he laid Goll's mangled foot gently on the floor, rose, stepped to the hearth and sat there, looking into the embers, smiling his little smile, while Goll dragged himself away.

After several moments of amazed silence, the onlookers gradually regained command of their voices, and the noise rose and rose again until someone shouted thirstily, 'Where's the *poitín?* Anyone'd want a good slug o' that stuff to steady his nerves after what we saw here tonight.' It was a suggestion that was to have evil consequences, especially for lovers of that same brew.

In answer, someone, trying to be helpful, bawled out, 'I know where 'tis! I'll bring it in.' Out he went, amid yells and whistles of approval.

But in order to get to the place where the *poitín* was, he had to pass the room where Clancy lay stiff amid the mourners, and as he rushed past the door he was suddenly throttled by strong hands and dragged into a dim corner. In a moment he was surrounded by none other than the three druids. Taoscán eyed him furiously, his face made even more dangerous-looking by the light of the lamp he carried.

'Where are you going, and what is afoot in there in that dark sty?' Taoscán jabbed a finger towards the hall, where the clamour of raucous noises could be clearly heard.

The messenger, by no means drunk, made an instant decision to answer the second question first. He could do that without lying, for woe betide the man discovered telling an untruth to a druid, and more so entirely to the chief druid of all Ireland.

'Ammm . . . your honour . . . they're only celebrating our beloved Emperor's journey into the next world. Sure, if he couldn't hear the voices of his friends behind him as he leaves for new lands to conquer, he might lose his courage entirely, or worse again, lose his way with looking behind him to find whether anyone was thinking of him at all.'

Taoscán stared at the fellow intently in that dim place. But he was speaking no heresy, only what everyone there, himself included, held as their firm belief.

'Hmph!' he growled. 'Better to let all that to us and the keening-women, maybe,' but he stepped aside, let the fellow proceed on his way and re-entered the dead-room, as did the other two, to continue with their praying over Clancy.

Sweating, the man made his way, carefully now, to a little room where he knew that several extra barrels of fine old *poitín* had been stored earlier in cooling mosses for just such an emergency as this. At the door, he called two passing servants to him and passed out a keg to each. 'Carry these down to the hall, quick, or there'll be trouble,' he told them. 'They're running dry.'

The servants eyed each other, smirked, but obeyed silently. Then he swung a keg onto his own shoulder and strode after them.

He reached the door only a few steps behind them, and heard the shrieks of delight as those inside saw what was coming. He began to run, mindful of the druid's anger, and only relaxed when the hall door thudded shut behind him.

Another chorus of whistles and whoops greeted his entry, even though he tried his best to quieten them: 'Shut up, can't ye! Ye'll bring them druids in on top of us, an' then there'll be crying in earnest.'

He might as well have been talking to the wall. The only hope – and that a slim one – of getting any silence at all, he knew, was to distribute the *poitín* – and quick.

That was done. The kegs were tapped at once and sent on their journey around the hall: one left, one right, and the third down the centre. No one bothered to pour the drink into goblet or cup, only put the tap to his mouth and sucked a *steall* from it. And no fear that any drinker was allowed more than five seconds' sucking. A vicious dig in the ribs awaited any greedy one that attempted it: 'Hi! D'you think there's anyone here but yourself? Pass it on, or I'll throttle you.'

And so the *poitín* did its round, amid a lull in the noise and jollity that amounted almost to silence. And all might yet have ended in good order and fellowship, had not someone just then called for cheese: 'Where is it, the *cáis?* What kind of a feast is this, without a bit o' cheese to wash down the drink?'

A pause. Then giggles and titters. Obviously the man had drunk more than was good for him and was getting confused. But he had made a valid point. Where *was* the cheese? And why had it to be called for? After all, at every funeral feast in the five corners of Ireland, never mind that of the Emperor of Corca Baiscinn, cheese was one of the staples provided for guests. And why? Because the best of good feeding was in it, and in every part of the land a different variety was made, each subtly distinct. It was a local way of saying 'We're here, an' we're us.' And for an important occasion like this, it was the woman of the house who supervised the work of making it, and making sure it was available – and enough of it – for the guests, no matter how many of them arrived.

And if every last scrap of it was not eaten, it was taken as a great insult, both to the hostess and to the dead. Not to eat it was the same as saying to the wife, 'You can't make cheese', and to the dead one, 'You hadn't much of a wife', so the custom was to eat it regardless. Most often, though, it never came to threats, for Irish cheese at that time was known to be the best in the world – a welcome addition at king's court or pauper's hovel. So, once the word was now mentioned, there was a loud clamour for it to be brought in.

Clancy's chief steward – who had hoped to profit by

selling the cheese later on the quiet – was now forced to act, and quickly too, for tables were beginning to dance and shudder under chorus after chorus of fist-blows.

'All right! All right, blast ye!' he snarled, and ordered three servants to hurry and bring in a large platter of cheese each quick, before objects of furniture began to fly.

It was a timely thought, and for good measure he borrowed another keg of mature *poitín,* 'Just to keep 'em occupied,' as he put it.

When all these items had been delivered to the hall and the door had been closed, Taoscán, who had taken a breather from praying and stood now in the corridor, watching, snorted angrily, 'Isn't there enough trouble awaiting people in this world, without searching it out?' It would have taken very little encouragement at that moment to make him step into their midst and put an end to the hilarity and noise with words of anger and power, as he had done many times before.

And it was a pity he chose not to, for just then things within were beginning to take a dark turn. And it was the cheese that did it. For every lover of *poitín* knows that cheese should never, ever be eaten with that drink – at least not if foul air is in any way strenuously objected to.

Who it was that let off the first explosion of personal wind no one could tell, since no one heard it over the general hubbub. But it was only the first of many. And far from being disgusted, most of the feasters let out whoops of laughter and encouragement, then leaned sideways on their hams and contributed their own efforts. Within ten minutes, the noise level had risen alarmingly into hilarious uproar.

'Whew! You dirty animal, Ó Murchú. No more of it, or you'll destroy your trousers.'

'By the Lord Lugh, you're good at it yourself, Ó Néill. You'd be a great man on board ship on a calm day!'

'Someone'll burst a gut. That's what I'm worried about,' added one of the Ó Laois, betraying his medical background.

And so on, and on, the air getting thicker and more foul by the minute. One by one, the lights began to flicker and die, and it was this growing darkness that gave O'Quinn his opportunity of the night. For that last barrel of *poitín* was coming slowly towards him down along the table, and when at last it was passed into his eager hands, he had no intention of letting it go until he had done it justice enough.

He raised it to his head, and – 'Glug-glug-glug' – refused to pass it on or heed any of the worried voices from the table down ahead of him, until the man next to him gave him a vicious *súnc* into the ribs. 'What the hell d'you mean, you greedy beast! Is it so you don't want any o' the rest of us to have a drop?'

'Hold your hour,' drooled O'Quinn. 'Can't ye see I'm busy,' and off he went, 'Glug-glug-glug' again.

Another, even more vicious, dig into the ribs, and – 'Unnghh!' – the keg spun out of his grasp, over his left shoulder, and spilt into staves on the ground. The precious *poitín* splashed over the floor between the tables, amid frenzied yells: 'Stop it!' and 'Don't let it go to waste!'

Within seconds, there was a crush of bodies, as men jumped, crawled and slithered to the spot, all dignity thrown aside, and began to lap, lick or feverishly suck in the fumes.

They were still at it when someone singled out O'Quinn. 'You! You're the cause of all this misfortune. Wasted the best thing we had tonight!'

And before O'Quinn could speak a word in reply, fists were flying. He was struck a vicious blow on the nose and collapsed backwards with a yell, blood squirting from both nostrils. He leaped up immediately, a dangerous-looking dagger in his left fist, and lunged at his attacker.

Luckily, Fionn saw it in time. 'Isn't it amazing, the way the bad blood breaks out in these fellows when the drop o' drink begins to work on 'em,' he thought, stepping quickly between them. It was just as well he did. The knife connected with his breastplate, screeched along it in a line of sparks, and O'Quinn stumbled awkwardly and lost his balance. Fionn grasped him by the scruff of his neck before he could hit the floor, and shook him. 'Calm down, my friend,' Fionn said to him. 'None o' that ugly stuff here – if you want to see the Glens of Antrim again.'

But now that his temper was up, O'Quinn would hear no reason. He squirmed, made a vicious tooth-snap at Fionn's wrist, and when Fionn, to avoid a wound – and infection, maybe – dropped him like a piece of dung, he landed, bounced instantly to his feet, jumped five feet into the air and, with a battle yell – 'Ya-eeee-aaaggh!' – that froze everyone in that hall, he stamped on Fionn's feet, driving them almost six inches into the floor.

It was a bad mistake. Fionn gasped, almost roared, but held it in. Then, with a snarl – 'Nnnggh!' – his hands clamped onto O'Quinn's neck. He could, there and then, have crushed the life from his opponent, separated head from body, but instead he plucked him from where he stood, swung him once around, then flung him. Direction was of no importance. Only temper.

'Ayeee-aaa . . . aaa!' For the only time in his life, O'Quinn flew, then connected with the wall and crumpled to the floor, followed by a shower of plaster.

The silence that followed lasted instants only. Then the men who had come south with him leaped to their feet, shouting for more blood.

'*Ochón!* Our beloved chief is down!'

'O'Quinn is scattered.'

'Murder! Revenge! Kill everyone!'

Within minutes, a serious battle was under way in the gloom. Diarmaid, Goll, Conán – all were drawn in one after the other, if only to defend themselves, for weapons were working in earnest now and the clash of blades mingled with shrieks and croaks, the heavy thump of falling bodies, and flying furniture landing.

Fionn did his best to halt this lunacy, but even his famed barrack-square voice was no match for the confusion that was now shaking the very walls and foundations of Dún Mór. Most of the people in the corridor outside, in the yard and in all the nearby rooms twitched nervously and licked their lips in fear, but a few were already running towards the fray armed with axes, cleavers and slashers, full of intent to make their mark. It was one of these who collided with Taoscán as he rushed, enraged, from the dead-room, the other two druids directly at his heels.

'Oh . . . oh, sorry, your honour. I . . . am . . . '

'What in the walls o' the world is happening?' shouted Taoscán. 'Is it an earthquake, or what?'

'No, your reverence, only a grand big fight in the hall. I'm going in to help.' Already there were several more behind him now, their weapons gleaming wickedly in the half-light.

Taoscán turned to Theosofix. 'Well? What do you think of our death-customs now, eh?'

'Interesting. Very interesting indeed,' nodded the man from Gaul.

'But ugly too,' snapped Taoscán. 'And this is one there'll be an end to right now.'

He warned the armed men back – they dared not disobey him – then led the other two druids to the door of the hall and listened.

Shrieks, groans and snarls. Hammering, heavy crashes and thumping. Howls of agony. Then more of the same.

'Merciful heavens protect us,' whispered Taoscán. 'In there must be the nearest thing in this world to the Black Pit, to hell itself. They'll wake the dead.'

'Do something . . . please,' begged Fraoch, 'before they wreck the *dún* entirely.'

'Indeed I will,' he hissed grimly. 'Get ready. We will enter all together.'

That they did: they pushed in the doors before them and stood there silent on the threshold. What met their eyes was a picture of insanity itself. No battlefield since the second battle of Moytura had seen anything like it. There were men in every stage of trying to live and of being killed in that room: some being jumped on, some bitten or twisted to death. There were eyes being picked out, brains being gnawed, legs and arms flung in every direction.

The walls, floor and furniture were splattered red and other colours – what remained of the furniture, that is. Heads were being hammered off walls, floor, fireplace, teeth being sunk anywhere they could do damage. And all this was taking place within a din, an uproar, in which voices were lost, even Fionn's. For he was still standing there like an oak tree, cracking heads together, tossing men aside like rag dolls, but being completely unheeded, though it was obvious to the frightened lookers-in at the door that he was bellowing at the top of his voice.

'This has gone far enough,' Taoscán snorted angrily when they had stood there for some time without the least effect. He stalked in, followed as usual by the others, and lit a taper so that their grey cloaks might be seen. After that, respect would do the rest, he knew.

Under normal circumstances it might have, but not now. The light merely made them a target, and in seconds, objects were showering in their direction. It was a piece of furniture that did the damage, though. Taoscán had just ducked – the indignity of it! – to avoid a stool flung in from somewhere on the left-hand side, but Theosofix was not so quick. It struck him just under the ear, and down he went with a small gurgle, a mere 'Ugkk!'

Fraoch jumped at once, out of this cursed place, back to the corridor, where a crowd was now gathered, peering in. But Taoscán stood his ground, shocked though he was.

'Reason is wasted on beasts like these within,' he fumed, 'so *draíocht* it will have to be.' With not a moment's more hesitation, he raised his hands (ducking several more flying objects as he did so) and recited in a strange, flat voice '*Ortha na dTrí bhFuacht*' – 'the Spell of the Three Freezings'. *'Fógraím oraibh fuacht na gcat, fuacht na linne 's fuacht úr-bhrat,'* and other words known only to himself, he uttered.

He was hardly finished when an extraordinary thing began to happen in that hall. Those within, no matter what they were doing at that moment, started to shiver, their teeth to chatter, their very blood to freeze.

But Taoscán had no opportunity to enjoy his handiwork, for just then there was a flurry at the door and several women dashed in, Clancy's wife and some of the keeners among them. They gathered on their knees round about Theosofix and stared at his still, pale face.

Clancy's wife rose then, slowly, her face twisted in anger. 'Savages!' she bawled. 'Animals! Ye have desecrated my husband's funeral and dishonoured our house. But now – *olagón ó!* – this druid is dead as well. A visitor to our land, too, here to honour us with his presence. My curse on the whole lot o' ye, no matter what rank ye hold.'

Taoscán's hand flashed out as she said these last words, his fingers snapped closed and he slowly lowered his fist until it was only inches from her face. She could see the fingers moving, as if something within was struggling to break free. 'No!' he scowled. 'No cursing at a funeral. Take back those words you spoke now – quickly!'

Frightened, she did so, and his fingers became still again. He opened his hand. Several black objects, like dead flies, tumbled to the floor. There they lay, unmoving.

'Good,' he nodded. 'There is no need of those here. Now, observe.' He beckoned towards the hall. And what an amazing change was there. Though teeth, fingers, knees were knocking and shaking within, every eye was on them at the doorway. All the noise of battle had died away, except for groanings here and there.

And now, while it was quiet, was the time, Taoscán decided, to make a most important announcement. He spoke slowly, quietly. 'If I suspend the spell that is now on ye, do ye promise to listen carefully to what I have to say?'

A frantic nodding of heads.

'And more importantly, will ye obey any orders I give?'

More nodding.

'Very well. But if I have to put one other spell on ye to bring back some sense of honour, there will be no lifting it.'

Utter silence.

Then, in that same strange, level voice, he snapped the spell in pieces: *'Ortha, stad. Éirigh. Imigh!'*

And the chattering, knocking, shivering stopped. At once.

But what of Theosofix? Was he dead or alive? Fionn, as well as the women, was kneeling by him now, peering anxiously. 'Lights here!' he shouted. They were brought and, by the flickering wicks, the still figure was examined. There was no blood, but he was as pale as death, his eyes shut. Not a sign of life was there.

Fionn rose, shaking with wrath. 'Who did this deed? He'll die tonight, the same person.'

No one owned up, naturally. Anyone who admitted to striking a druid would be cast out from all civilized society and treated like a leper.

Three times, Fionn's fierce eyes raked the company, from left to right and back again. But still no one responded. He spoke then, a tremor in his voice.

'By my honour and the honour o' the Fianna, I'll have an answer to my question before anyone leaves here tonight. I'm amazed at ye. Is there no honour at all left among the chieftains of Ireland any more?'

No answer.

'Someone looking at me now killed a holy man here this night, an' every one o' ye is shamed until that person is found. Ye don't seem to understand that.'

Just then, there was a stir down the hall, and a tall, dangerous-looking warrior, one of the O'Connors of Sligo, jostled his way to the front. He faced Fionn squarely. 'Part o' the fault o' this is your own, Fionn Mac Cumhail. You an' your men were in the fight as good as anyone else.'

'Me?' Fionn almost shouted.

'Yes, you. Look.' He pointed to Fionn's right hand. And sure enough, there, clutched still between his fingers, was a clump of hair which he had torn from someone's head.

He shook it from him in disgust, just as one of the O'Carrolls of Ely made himself heard. ''Twas that cursed *poitín* that did it. It should be let into no house during a wake.'

'Or a wedding, either,' added another wise one.

Much nodding of heads.

'I'm telling ye this much here an' now,' Fionn announced then. 'Wherever I'm at a wake from this night onward – or any other member of the Fianna, either – there'll be no more *poitín.*'

'Good, good,' smiled Taoscán, stepping forward now. 'I'll pass on that very message to King Cormac at Tara, and new laws will be drawn up very soon. Games on their own, yes. Drink on its own, maybe, in moderation. But games and drink and cheese together, no. Never again.'

More enthusiastic nodding.

'In a way, I am sorry to hear it,' came a faint voice from behind them.

They froze an instant, then wheeled about – just in time to see Theosofix rise shakily to his knees, rubbing his ear as he did so.

'Merciful heavens, is it a ghost?' gurgled Goll.

Already two servants were helping the druid to his feet.

'No ghost,' he frowned unsurely. 'Only myself . . . I think.'

He was surrounded at once by mightily relieved well-wishers, each one anxious to touch him, congratulate him.

'I am well,' he smiled. 'But I am sorry to see an old custom dismissed because of me.'

Taoscán stepped forward now, firmness in his voice. 'What is agreed is agreed. But that is no reason why the same must be done in Gaul.'

'Just as well,' said Theosofix. 'I could never see my countrymen agree to give up drinking at all public celebrations – maybe more's the pity.'

*

For the short remainder of that night (it was almost dawn by then), there was much earnest talk of what had happened, the kind of lunacy that had gripped them all, as well as great exertion by the druids and Ó Laoi to patch up the injured. But there was no more drink drunk – except spring water. And how welcome it was after the firewater that had gone before.

'Ahhh! That's the stuff. Good for the heart an' good for the brain,' said someone.

'If we'd started with that,' another added, 'maybe our heads wouldn't be opening an' shutting now . . . Ooo-uuu!'

And for the remaining two nights of the wake, things continued so. At least something good had come out of the death of Boethius Clancy.

But no one could deny that the only ones who survived that first night's horrible doings with their reputations wholly intact were the druids and keeners. They, at least, had done their duty by the dead.

And so it was only fitting, when at last Clancy was carried, feet first, down the long road to his imperial resting place, that they should have pride of place directly behind his wife. The druids, in their grey cloaks, and the women, with their cries of mourning, lent dignity to the funeral, in spite of the fact that the man they were burying was one who in his lifetime had neither respect for nor belief in gods, the past or anything to do with the other world.

Whatever about all that, it was a noble send-off, and for many generations – centuries, even – afterwards, as a result of the promises made on that fateful night, the good habit took root, grew and persisted of conducting such occasions as wakes, weddings, funerals and all great gatherings of state in sobriety and with decorum – which gave to the land of Ireland a reputation for steadiness, piety and good sense unrivalled in all the known world.

All of which, sadly, we stand in danger of losing in this modern age of affluence, plenty and senselessness.

Fionn Mac Cumhail and Taoscán Mac Liath would hardly be impressed.

FIONN MAC CUMHAIL
AND THE BRAIN-BALL FACTORY

Fighting wars, in Ireland or anywhere else, has never been a pretty thing. But at least, by the time that Fionn Mac Cumhail and the Fianna were keeping order in the land, many of its worst and most savage features had been got rid of: evils like eating the hearts of enemies, still warm on the field of battle, using their skulls as wine cups, making necklaces of dried-up fingers, and other such things.

It must not be thought, of course, that it was the fighting men who gave up these filthy customs. Or their so-called betters, either – the kings and lords of the land. No, it was the druids of Ireland who, gradually, in a series of great meetings (such as the Convention of Carn Mór, the Convocation of Maigh Chuilinn and the Council of Cashel, to name only a few), brought some sense of near-civilisation to the constant warfare that the Irish loved almost above life itself. Extracting teeth as souvenirs from the wounded was forbidden, as was the cutting off of ears and noses, as well as all kinds of cannibalism.

'Damn it, but sure what's the good in fighting if all the fun is taken out of it!' was the predictable response from those who should have had sense, but alas, never had – i.e. the princes of the land.

'At least now, maybe my corpse'll get a decent burial an' I won't be walking the other world searching for bits o' me,' was the more sensible reaction of most ordinary sword-warriors and hatchet-men.

But as they themselves well knew, the druids could only gradually bring their civility to all corners of the land. There were many throwbacks to the bad former times, and even the most honourable of fighters would sometimes, in the heat of battle, revert to old vile habits and low-life practices. But overall, at the annual druids' meeting held at Beann Éadair in the fourteenth year of the reign of Cormac as High King, the chief druid, Taoscán Mac Liath, had been able to announce further steady progress.

'It gives me great pleasure to say that in the past twelve months, fewer people than ever before have been eaten alive in the land of Ireland, and no more than a score or two impaled – and those for evil deeds worthy of the punishment. And it is most pleasant of all not to hear' – he gave a little smile at this – 'about any eating of human brains – except among the O'Farrells, and their land is so beggarly that they might almost be forgiven such a horrible deed.'

This last change gave him particular pleasure, for he had, during his long career, made a deep study of his fellow humans and had concluded that the human spirit resided in the head. And since the brain also filled the head – he had seen all too many examples of split skulls after battles – then it must follow that the spirit was contained in the brain. Hence his long battle to have the heads of the dead respected. 'Otherwise the spirit will be forced to wander,' the druid would say. 'And everyone, I think, fears the wandering dead. And not without reason, either.'

All of these gradual changes for the better were accompanied by another change, of course: in the weapons by which all these terrible injuries were inflicted. Step by step, and against fierce opposition, the weapons of war were classified: their weight, their size, who could carry what, and when. There was terrific hullabaloo, naturally, when each new regulation was proclaimed, but as each was seen to be for the benefit of everyone, especially the fighters themselves, they came to be accepted and, more importantly, the good sense of the druids' council became more and more a matter of common knowledge.

When it was decided at the Droma Riasc meeting that offensive weapons would henceforth be confined to seven types – swords, knives, spears, axes, slings, hammers and brain-balls – no one objected. 'If you can't kill your enemy with one or more o' them, you should be looking after sheep, not fighting,' was the general consensus.

But there were some people – the more thinking ones – who raised their eyebrows when the list was published. 'The first six, yes, maybe,' these people said. 'But why did Taoscán leave brain-balls in it? Sure, don't everyone know his fondness an' care for the human brain.' It was an acute observation. Even King Cormac was surprised, though he asked no questions.

It eventually fell to Fionn to find out what everyone else wished to discover –and he did so partly by accident. For one thing was clear in all these new upheavals in society: it was not to be expected that the reforms would go unquestioned, even among the druids themselves.

For instance, there was Dearbhnán, an opinionated, pompous druid from the O'Donnell country. 'Dearbhnán Draoi, the Ollamh of Uladh' he called himself – this written in large letters on his place of consultation, the oak grove of Doire Olc (he liked to portray himself as sinister!). His use of the title caused no little resentment among other Ulster druids, and among schoolmen and poets too. 'Them are titles he has no right or claim to,' they would say.

But Taoscán could not discipline Dearbhnán so easily, since he needed every vote he could muster to push through the battle reforms, especially concerning brain-balls. There was much wrangling and hair-splitting between the various factions, with, for instance, one of Dearbhnán's followers certain that the spirit of a person lay in the eyes: 'Aren't they always moving!'. Others were convinced that only the heart could contain the soul, and others again that it lay in the feet. Therefore, they insisted, brains could be disposed of with few consequences: 'An' anyway, didn't our ancestors use brain-balls back to the start o' the world, so why shouldn't we allow it too? Who may take it on himself to change a hallowed tradition such as that?'

Only very gradually (and with many bribes – 'favours', he called them) could Dearbhnán be persuaded at their next meeting in Teamhar Luachra to sign a further page that recommended to the High King that these weapons be outlawed.

Back at Tara, on his way home to Ulster, Dearbhnán spoke directly and boldly to Cormac. 'After the Droma Riasc proclamation, this will only confuse people entirely. Didn't we say there only a short time ago that brain-balls were to be allowed? O'Donnell won't like this, or Maguire either, or O'Hanlon – not to mention O'Neill and several more I could name.'

'What you'll do now is tell 'em that *I* won't like *them* if they don't heed this new proclamation,' Cormac replied sharply, handing him the piece of paper. 'An' make sure 'tis copied, distributed an' obeyed in all of Uladh.' At this, even Fionn looked twice. Was the king finally getting sense, or was he on the poitín again?

It was only later, when Fionn quietly read a copy of the proclamation, that he saw the reason for his master's stern words and Dearbhnán's objections:

> Be it known to one and all within the five Corners of Ireland that I, Cormac, Lord of land and sea, from the sky's height to the farthest horizon's edge, do command it done that from Lá Bealtaine next brain-balls cease to be used in any manner of fight or dispute whatsoever. On the urgent advice of the council of druids is this done, so that any further dishonour to the human spirit may be avoided.
>
> The making, trading or having of all such loathsome objects will cease from the time that this proclamation is displayed.
>
> Let it be done!
>
> Cormac Rex

'Hmm! That'll get their backs up in Uladh all right,' Fionn muttered to Liagán Luaimneach later on the battlements, repeating what he had read. He well knew that it was only with the utmost surliness that most of the chiefs mentioned could even be got to acknowledge Cormac as High King. Without the Fianna to press his claim, Cormac would scarcely have got a single cow in tribute from that province.

'Bit of exercise for us, if nothing else,' giggled Liagán. He had a habit of giggling, but behind that seeming silliness lurked a warrior who was as strong as ten men – and from whom it was best to flee when battle-rage was on him. 'Still, this is no kind o' weather for settling arguments in.'

And that seemed a sensible observation, for as he spoke it was a grey drizzling evening in November and the torches had been lit on the watch-towers of Tara. He was looking out gloomily over the ramparts, towards the west. Nothing was stirring – not even the smoke, it seemed – nor was there any sound except the snuffling of a guard and the drip-drop of rain from the thatch.

He shook himself and shivered. 'Maybe Taoscán might be doing something interesting below in his workshop. Come on, we'll go down. Anything'd be better than freezing here.'

He vaulted from the high walkway down into the yard, not bothering with the ladder, and nodded to the perished guards as the side-gate was opened to let them out. In minutes they were at the foot of the hill, and they found Taoscán's door open even on such a miserable evening.

The old man was busy, as always, among his beloved jars, herbs and vellums, muttering distractedly, as if he had lost something important. Fionn was about to turn at the door and wait for a more opportune time, but Taoscán spotted him. 'Ah, just the man I was wanting to see! And welcome to you, too, Liagán. Only proper that you should hear what I have to say as well, if you wish.' He motioned them in. 'Find a place, if ye can.'

They were careful not to disturb the cluttered pages, jars and potions as they searched out a spot to fit themselves, for well they knew that each and every scrap here inside might have in it the power of life and death for someone – and even worse, death-in-life. As they had witnessed all too often.

'Now, Fionn, I can guess the purpose of your visit on this dark evening,' Taoscán said, and he smiled his little ghost of a smile. 'Would it have anything to do with the proclamation this day gone out from His Highness?'

'It would indeed,' Fionn nodded. 'You know yourself, Taoscán, that trouble is going to follow it, especially in Uladh. Did you hear what Dearbhnán had to say?'

'I did.'

'An' does it give you no worry?'

'Who do you think wrote the proclamation in the first place?'

'I can guess – yourself,' Fionn said. 'It has your voice in it.'

'You guess correctly.' Taoscán rose now and began to pace the floor, his hands clasped behind him. 'It was the only way. Make the thing come to the fore. Otherwise Dearbhnán would always have one more objection. We would never reach an end.'

'That's fine to say,' growled Fionn, 'but 'tis me an' the Fianna that'll have to face the music when the trouble starts. There's stubborn an' awkward lads up there in the forests an' bogs of Uladh. Only looking for trouble, usually, an' here are we, giving 'em the very excuse they need.'

Taoscán stopped, and looked at them steadily. 'Do you know . . . have you any notion of all the brave warriors and others who at this moment are staggering through the dark shades of the other world, injured beyond telling even there, always searching, clawing for peace, for rest they can never have? And all because of those cursed brain-balls! Night after night, they keep me awake here, begging to be released from the pain, the terror, of being two persons in one or, worse again, not knowing are they human or animal, all because evil-minded wretches have used the brain of a pig, a hound or – vile thought! – a wolf in the making of those hellish articles. Bad enough it is, as you well know, to face the walking things of this world in the dark. But ten times – no, a hundred times – worse, to face the walkers of the other world, to hear their shrieks and be able to help so few. It pains me even to think of them.'

The glint in his eye was dangerous now. 'And every day their number is added to by the makers of those filthy, evil weapons – if they could even be called that!'

He pounded the table here, set his various bits and pieces jumping. The noise seemed to have a sobering effect on him, though. He sighed, then looked away. 'Forgive me. It is a subject that keeps me from all calmness. But now' – he shook his head – 'the reason I hoped you would visit me is this: in the days and weeks to come, there will be trouble as His Majesty's proclamation is spread throughout the land, make no mistake of that.'

'What kind o' trouble?' Liagán asked.

'Dark deeds. Threats. Ignoble acts. Attacks. And they will be cowardly, be sure of it. Those who supply brain-balls in great quantities will not lightly see their business destroyed.'

Fionn sat on the window ledge now, for want of a better place. Liagán warmed his rear end to the fire.

Fionn licked his lips, breathed heavily, thought a moment. 'You won't mind me saying this, I hope, Taoscán. But you know as well – what am I saying! – you know a lot *better* than me that these brain-balls are like *poitín*. People in this land of Ireland have used 'em since before anyone can even . . . even count back to. How can you hope to change habits that go down into the darkness of time?'

Taoscán stopped pacing, stared at the wall a moment, then swung around towards Fionn. 'The problem with this land of ours is that the mists and rain seem to throw a blight on men's thinking also. Those words you spoke only now, can you say for sure they are true?'

'Well . . . no . . . but . . . everyone knows – '

'Everyone does *not* know!' There was a sharpness, an anger even, in Taoscán's voice that was foreign to him.

Fionn only shrugged. 'No offence meant, Taoscán, but – '

'And none taken,' snapped the old man. 'But let me tell you something now – both of you – which will have to be learned sooner or later by everyone of understanding (and such are few, indeed) in this land if we are ever to rid the world of this foulness. The old lie that using brain-balls is one of our traditions must be laid to rest. Understand this: killing of any persons I am not allowed to approve of, nor do I, though it has always been in the world. And will always be. Human nature is thus and will not change. But there are violent ways in which one can die that make no difference to that person in the next world. Such death is' – he shrugged, and then his voice stiffened – 'is infinitely to be preferred to the plague that Miocnait Maslach brought with him from his cursed land of Thessaly when he was washed ashore at Inbhear Scéine during the great autumn storm of Conaire Mór's reign.'

Fionn and Liagán were staring at Taoscán now, as if he were speaking of a foreign place and time. 'You're . . . amm . . . kind o' leaving me lost, Taoscán,' Fionn breathed apologetically. 'I don't know a thing about what you're saying there, but if you say it, I believe it.'

There was a pause. It was Liagán who broke it. 'But Taoscán, if you don't mind me asking – an' I'm only a poor ignorant man, so excuse me for saying it – was it a disease he brought, that lad, or what?'

The old man stopped, then slapped his hands on his knees. 'Good! Good! You're not as ignorant as you say, Liagán. No!' And he became serious again. 'What Miocnait brought was this gross custom of using the brains of those killed in honourable battle to kill other warriors.'

Fionn almost laughed here. 'We learned his habit very quick, didn't we!'

Taoscán nodded sadly. 'That much I must admit. But perhaps it is not too late to change.' The sigh he let out then might have given an observer some reason for pause, but he continued, still solemn, but more lightly now. 'What most people today do not know – how could they? – is that it is not the brains that are used in the brain-balls that matters most. They do matter, of course, as I told you already, and very much so. But equally important is how they are mixed, with what, and with what words. Not everyone can do it, believe me.'

'I *do* believe you,' Fionn nodded, 'but explain a bit more, will you?'

'It is too complicated in all its detail, but let me tell you this much: the one in charge of making the most lethal of these brain-balls, the one who sets the dead walking, knows well what he is about. Especially if he has the knowledge of the *dób.*'

'The *dób?*' repeated Liagán. 'What d'you mean? I'm not following you.'

'Many a learned man would not,' smiled Taoscán, not at all insultingly. 'You see, the *dób buí* that is used for holding together the mixture of brain, blood and water can come from one of three places only. The water must be measured exactly, and must be taken from the joining of seven streams at the full of the moon. That alone has the power required to put victims beyond the help even of my art.'

'An' these three places, now, where the *dób* must be got,' murmured Fionn, quick of mind, as always, 'wouldn't it make sense to put 'em in a way that they couldn't be used for this kind o' villainy?'

'Well thought of,' smiled Taoscán. 'But there is a difficulty. As you know, many people make their livelihood from the using of *dób* – for walls, floors and much more. And it is so even in those three special places. Nine-tenths of all the *dób* that is mined in each of them is harmless and may be used safely by anyone. But in each of them, and in no other of the many places where *dób* is found, there is a thin layer – not more than a fingernail's thickness – of *dób dearg.* That is where the danger lies, for *dób dearg* in the hands of him who knows its power is not alone dangerous, but frightful in its consequences.'

'But what *is* that red stuff?' Liagán asked, mystified. 'Where did it come from?'

Taoscán did not reply at once. He seemed to be considering something. When at length he spoke, it was with care. 'If I told you, Liagán, that I had an answer to that, it might make you feel better, even safer. But I will tell no lies here tonight. I do not know. It is something I have given much thought to. While both of you, and the others above' – he nodded towards Tara's battlements – 'have been about your business throughout the land, I have sat here night after night questioning these same small details, that have such frightful consequences. The question is always the same: "Why?" The answers are rarely so simple. I could tell you what I *think* it is. But that would be opinion only, and my opinion could be contradicted by many others.'

Fionn rose now. 'If you say 'tis such – whatever that might be – I'll stand behind you, no matter who else talks.'

'An' me,' added Liagán.

Taoscán smiled. 'To know that gives me more pleasure than you may realise. But the fact still remains, I cannot be wholly sure.'

'We realise that,' Fionn agreed, 'but we'd still like to hear what you think.'

Taoscán breathed deeply, blinked, then spoke to the ceiling, calmly, slowly. 'There must have been a time, way back, thousands of years ago – maybe even more – when a deed of such terrible violence, with such shedding of blood, occurred that the earth was soaked in it. I can only think that the gods were so incensed . . . angered' – he saw that they did not understand the first word he had used – 'that they buried this horror from the sight of all who were to follow. What they may have done to those responsible, I cannot say. But in the silence of many a night, I feel the echoes of it even yet and fear it in its awfulness.'

They could see from his taut cheeks, his mirthless lips, his very motionlessness, that there was more here than they would ever come to grips with – or have need to, thanks be to the kind Lugh! 'Who'd want to be a druid?' was the thought uppermost in both their minds then. 'Isn't it bad enough to have to deal with troubles you can see, not to mind the ones that are invisible.' But their thoughts were interrupted by –

'Whatever about its origin, its results are all too clear to see. And the time has come for it to be suppressed.'

'Well, if you'll tell us where these three places are, we'll do whatever we can to put a stop to this trade once an' for all,' growled Fionn. 'If only to improve your night's sleep.' And he grinned.

'There is more than that in question here,' nodded Taoscán, 'but that would be a helpful consequence, right enough.'

'So . . . tell us.'

'The first of them is in the county of Ciarraí, at a place beside the little river Claodach at Brosnach. A lonesome place, I can tell you. The second is at Poll Buí, near Béal Átha na Sluaigh, which you all know. And the third is on the shore of Loch Neacach. This is where most of the *dób dearg* comes from – more than ten times the amount of the two others combined. If that can be controlled, the rest will be easy.'

Fionn scratched his beard. 'I thought there was nothing in that lake but eels.'

'Yes, they are there too, but they cause bother to no man, only feed many. It is the *dób* that makes the difference, and the rulers of Dál nAraide were not long in finding out its value, especially Maelgarbh.'

'Him?' answered Liagán. 'Oh, he would surely. One o' the most miserable men that ever stumbled the earth. Too mean even to feed himself, not to mind his family.' Liagán obviously had no love for the same Maelgarbh, whatever the reason.

'True,' replied Taoscán, 'but his greed may make your task easier when you come to . . . ah . . . talk with him – or better again, with the one who is his ally in all this.'

Fionn grinned. 'If we have to go there, there'll be more done than talking, I can promise you that.'

'I don't doubt you, but care will be necessary. As I will explain.'

'Just tell us which end o' the lake to go to, an' we'll do the rest.'

It was Taoscán's turn to smile. He could not but admire their fearlessness. He knew, though, that the same hasty bravery had all too often led them into situations which they were ill-equipped to handle. He did not want that to happen here. 'I will do that, never fear. But more, too . . . more . . .'

He seemed weary all of a sudden. Fionn noticed it, too. He jumped off the window ledge. 'Are you all right, Taoscán?'

The old man's fingers were pressed to his temples, his eyes closed tight, as if he were trying to squeeze something urgent out of his head – something that they needed to hear. In a few moments his eyes opened, his hands relaxed. 'I saw – or half-saw – something, Fionn, that could make all the difference to whether your journey north is successful or not.'

'Good, good. Tell us.'

'Indeed I will, but allow me time to think more about it first. You will not be kept waiting any longer than need be.'

They took the hint, and moved towards the door.

'If there's anything – '

'I know that very well, Fionn. But leave me now awhile to consider.'

They stepped out into the gloom and drizzle and began to climb the hill towards the gate, each one silent, revolving his own thoughts.

But before any explanations or directions came from Taoscán, a small incident occurred that made information from him quickly necessary, and then something else, which was far more serious and demanded immediate action. The first happened early the following day.

Just before dawn, Fionn had inspected the guards at each of the gates and spoken a few encouraging words (much-needed in this miserable weather) to the shivering soldiers before retiring for his usual three to four hours' sleep before Cormac began baying for his breakfast, for attention, for . . . Lugh knew what! Nothing was stirring. At each sentry station, the reply to his 'How goes it here?' was the same: 'Nothing stirring, Fionn.'

'I'm glad to hear it. Good morrow, then.' And he had retired, thinking, of course, on what Taoscán had said, but confident too that action would soon follow.

And it did. For he was hardly two hours in bed when his room door was rattled by loud knocking. 'Fionn! Fionn! Out of it, quick!' It was Diarmaid, and excited, too.

Fionn had barely sprung up in the bed when his friend was by his side, full of urgency. 'Wha – ? What's wrong?' Fionn exclaimed.

'Come out, quick! The north gate. Hurry, 'till you see what's there.'

In seconds, Fionn was shambling after him in his nightshirt, yawning, rubbing *breac* from his eyes, looking anything but the mighty hero, Ireland's great defender.

But when he arrived at the gate and stepped outside it, all dazedness left him, for there stood a semicircle of the Fianna, their attention focused on something hanging from the huge timberwork, so far as he could see. They were chattering among themselves, glancing all the while at the thing, but making no move towards it. Obviously they were waiting for his guidance. Fionn pushed through them, to within an arm's length of the object suspended there. A hush fell as he stared at it, examining it closely.

It was a piece of fabric, meshed like a fishing net and hanging from one of the great iron bars that held the oak timbers together. But that was a mere detail. Much more to the point was what the net contained: brain-balls. There could be no doubt of it. He moved even closer, counted them. Something . . . something was very wrong here. He was about to grasp the net and turn it about to make sure, when a voice at his ear hissed, 'Don't touch it! If you're seeing what I'm seeing, there's danger here. Send down for Taoscán.'

He snapped around. It was Diarmaid. Their eyes met

an instant, then Fionn nodded. 'Run, down, quick, Goll, to Taoscán,' Fionn said, turning to his friend. 'Tell him what's here – that we need him at once.'

That surly man turned and clumped off round the hillside. He, in spite of his roughness, was as anxious as all the others not to miss any detail of what this might mean.

By the time Taoscán came – and it was no long time – the crowd at the gate had increased to several dozen. But without a word, a path was opened for the druid.

He saluted no one, not even Fionn, only strode to the gate and looked long and steadily at what hung there. Then he drew out slowly, from the folds of his long tunic, a stick, no more than a foot in length, and delicately poked the net, turning it back to front and round again.

'That's no ordinary stick. Ancient oak, you can be sure,' whispered Conán to Liagán, who merely nodded, fascinated by what he was seeing. Rarely was it, indeed, that any of them had the opportunity of viewing the details of a druid's knowledge in action.

'You see what's here, Fionn, don't you?' Taoscán sighed.

'I do. Brain-balls.'

'Yes, but did you count them?'

'I couldn't. I was afraid to touch it' – eyeing Diarmaid here! – 'in case it might be a thing of evil.'

'And right you were in that. It was put here with the intention of – '

He got no further, for at that moment King Cormac bustled out the gate, still struggling with the sleeves of his royal red robe. 'What's here? What's all this fuss about?' he puffed. 'Whatever 'tis, ye can be calm now – I'm here.'

There were several spluttered guffaws behind hands,

quickly quelled by a dark glare from Fionn.

'Your Highness,' Fionn said, bowing slightly, 'Taoscán has something to show you that may interest you.' And he directed the High King towards where the old man was picking delicately at the net with his wand – for that is what it was: timeless, inherited, powerful.

Even Cormac was silent now, in the presence of what he at once knew he could not explain. And the silence lasted all of half an hour, while Taoscán did what he had to do – poked, measured, observed, but never once touched with his fingers the thing on the gate.

At last he turned and addressed them all clearly. 'There is no need for me to carry this' – he jerked his thumb at it, disgustedly – 'to where I examine most things of a like nature. I can tell you here what it is, where it came from.'

'Well, do,' snarled Cormac. 'Because the one that did this is dead already, even though we don't know yet who he is.'

'Hmmm . . . ' Taoscán pursed his lips. 'That may be, but I think it may take a little longer than that.'

'How so? Am I the High King, or am I not?!'

'Let us . . . ah . . . discuss this matter in a place where there is quietness', Taoscán said, smiling, and winked at Fionn, who immediately swung round and faced all those present.

'All right!' he bawled. 'Enough o' this idleness. What're ye doing here, anyway? Isn't there someplace that each one o' ye should be at this hour?'

They jerked briefly to attention, then began to slink off reluctantly. And Fionn saw that too, and felt sorry for them. After all, he himself would not, he knew, like to be excluded from something as mysterious as this. So he added, as they scattered, 'But have no fear. As soon as anything may be told of this, no one will know it before ye. I promise it.'

At that they brightened, knowing him to be a man strictly of his word.

When only four of them remained, Cormac, whose lips and fingers were twitching now with annoyance and impatience, snorted, 'All right, Taoscán, no more mystery about this! Tell us out what you know.'

And he did, with few words. *'Piseogs.* To frighten us. No more, no less.'

'Frighten us? Here at Tara? Why would they try a thing as stupid as that? Especially with you here.' It was Fionn who said it, but he was immediately interrupted by Cormac.

'If they want fight, 'tis fight they'll get, whoever they are!' he barked. 'I'll see to that much!'

'Who *are* they first?' breathed Fionn, his temper rising, but unable to say what he might have wished to his lord and master.

Taoscán smiled fleetingly, but answered deadly seriously. 'Who do you think? The crowd by Loch Neacach, of course. That proclamation did it. And how quickly! They feel threatened, so their answer is to threaten. The oldest reaction in the world.' He stepped to the gate, pointed to the net bag. 'I have examined these closely, and believe me, they were put together by no ignorant hands. The one who did it knew what he was about – and knew that I would know it.'

'But . . . what sort of a man would that be?'

'One who has profited from the filthy trade, and who still does, no doubt.'

There was a pause, as if no one wanted to make the first open accusation. Then Diarmaid asked, mildly, 'It wouldn't have anything to do with any o' the O'Neills, would it?'

'It would,' Taoscán answered gravely. 'Very, very much.'

Even Cormac stopped at this. Maelgarbh would be relatively easy to deal with, but the O'Neills were a different matter entirely. 'Which of 'em are you talking about? You know as well as I do that they're at three sides o' Loch Neacach. An' they're all related. A wild crowd. You'd want to be very sure o' who you're accusing there, or you'll bring the whole gang of 'em down on our heads.'

'Why do you think I asked for quietness and privacy to discuss this?' smiled Taoscán.

'I hope, as well as Maelgarbh, that 'tis the McGurks or the O'Devlins, or even the O'Laverys, that are behind this,' sighed Fionn. 'Maybe an O'Neill hand isn't in it at all.' He was clutching at straws, and he knew it.

Taoscán laughed drily. 'Not directly, maybe. It wasn't he that made the mixture for those brain-balls, but his druid did.'

'How can you tell that?'

'There isn't a druid in Ireland but I'd know him by the method of his mixing, whatever about the words he might use,' Taoscán replied. 'And I know this is the work of Dubhdraoi, whose lord is O'Neill of Clanna Buí. Maelgarbh is only a small man in all of this.'

'Well, that's it so, isn't it!' snapped Cormac. 'With an evil-sounding name like that, I'd believe it, too. What more proof do we need? Fionn, get the Fianna together an' teach him a lesson he'll never forget.'

'Wait . . . wait,' cautioned Taoscán. 'There's a better way. Why don't I write a letter to O'Neill first, asking him does he know what has been done in his name? And if we receive no reply in, say, four days, then Fionn can do whatever you demand.'

Fionn broke in here: 'An' that'll give us time to prepare ourselves properly for the worst, if it comes.'

Much against his will, Cormac had to agree. But little did any of them realise, as they parted at the gate, that something else would arrive to upset their plans before the letter, which was written and sent that very day, could be answered. And an impressive letter it was too, written in Taoscán's unique manner, conciliatory but firm, leaving O'Neill in no doubt about what was being done by his druid, and the consequences if an immediate stop was not put to it.

But the like *was* repeated. And worse. Within two days. With results that were far-reaching indeed. But it was the treachery of it that shocked all at Tara and ensured that there would be swift revenge, if that was within human reach.

Among the heroes of the Fianna, Fionn as leader made wide allowance for all kinds of habits and little oddnesses. 'As long as it don't interfere with what ye do in battle, 'tis fine with me', was his philosophy.

This was why Diarmaid was allowed to powder his cheeks (to attract the women), Conán not laughed at no matter what absurd attempts he made to hide his shining, sweaty baldness, or Liagán Luaimneach reprimanded when he, every Lá Bealtaine and Samhain, buried his head in seashore sand for fear of the *síógaí.* Fionn respected each man's private beliefs – and most of his warriors had some such.

Yet even he found it a constant matter for head-shaking when Siascán, one of his toughest, battle-scarred veterans, day after day, all year round, went hunting snails in his every free moment. They helped him against the *íseal brí,* he claimed. Not ordinary snails, either, but only those in yellow and brown shells. These he sought out, no matter where in Ireland he might be on campaign or visit, sucked them from their shells and swallowed them whole and raw. Then he would delicately replace each shell, unbroken, where he had found it.

'No point in disappointing that poor creature's family,' he was heard to say after one such eating, and from then on he was regarded as a man with a certain important part of his mind not altogether functioning. Yet, apart from giving him the nickname 'Siascán Seilmide', never a one interfered, for in any battle, even the fiercest, he had not once been found wanting.

So no one, two days later, took the slightest notice when Siascán stepped eagerly out the eastern gate, as he usually did in wet weather, his snail-bag on his back, unarmed except for a single dagger. The banks of the river were always good hunting grounds for him, though in weather like this the snails were easy to find in most fields. ('Coming into the beds to us, they are,' was Fionn's comment. 'Sure, any night I don't keep my mouth closed I have my breakfast before I get up.') Siascán would have none of this. He preferred them fresh from the grass, and that was that. And he usually came back, his appetite well satisfied and his bag full.

Yet on this day he did not return. No one noticed it at first, but when the second changing of the guards took place and there was still no trace of him, Lorcán Léime it was who thought to question the fact. He mentioned it to Fionn, who was doing his rounds of the four gates just then. 'Is Siascán inside, Fionn? He went out this morning, but anyone I talked to don't seem to have seen him since. Check it out, will you, when you have time.'

Fionn, at first, saw no reason to do that but, careful of details, as always at Tara, he mentioned it here, there, outside and inside the gates. No one had heard of or seen Seascán since his earlier going out.

'Unusual,' muttered Fionn. 'But maybe this time he ate too many o' them cursed snails.' He shuddered and laughed at the same time, then walked on, shrugging.

But the following morning, when Siascán had not put in an appearance for guard duty, Fionn decided enough was enough. 'Find him!' he ordered the sentries. 'He won't be gone too far. Ye know where to search.'

They did. And they found him, too, within twenty minutes. Crumpled beside a hedge, not a quarter of a mile from the eastern gate he had exited so happily the previous morning. His mouth was open, hanging foolishly, the whites of his eyes gleaming up, his fingers bunched. But what silenced and shocked those who found him was his head. It was split. They could see the forehead-bone broken even under the skin. Yet there was no wound.

Dlúthach was about to turn him over when Suibhne flung his hand forward. 'No! It'd be better to let Taoscán do the examining. Otherwise we're only making trouble for ourselves. I know it.'

Dlúthach straightened, inhaled deeply. 'All right. Get him.'

Within minutes, the spot was crowded, everyone voicing his disgust and anger at the sight of their friend sprawled dead.

When Taoscán arrived, Fionn and Diarmaid in step with him, there was silence, as before at the gate above. The old man looked down at the ugly sight, his face utterly still. Then he nodded, looked briefly away, as if it was an all-too-familiar sight to him. 'Fionn,' he said softly, 'turn him over, slowly. With a prayer, respectfully. And be mindful in particular of the head, for what concerns us most is there, beneath . . . within . . . Of that I have no doubt.'

These last words were uttered almost in a whisper, as though to himself. But Fionn heard them, for in that circle of warriors no one was moving or speaking. He beckoned to Diarmaid and between them they turned Siascán over, Diarmaid taking the body, Fionn clasping that shattered head uneasily but gently in his huge, hairy paws.

And there, just as Taoscán had predicted, Siascán's *poll* told all. The head was smashed, and bedded in it for all of them to see was . . . a brain-ball.

'If . . . if . . . 'twas his forehead itself . . . I mightn't object too much . . . '

Fionn had hardly stumbled out the words when Taoscán slammed down his left hand and swung around, eyes blazing. 'No! No!' His voice was like ice breaking. 'While that is the opinion here . . . here in Tara itself, there will be no end to this terrible evil. You, Fionn, you know what this man now faces in the other world. Have I not told you?' His face was white, his hands trembling.

Fionn backed away, genuinely fearful. 'I . . . ' He shook his head. 'I'm . . . so shocked to see Siascán like this that I . . . '

Taoscán relaxed, nodded. Then his head slumped forward, onto his chest. 'Humanity, humanity,' he thought. 'Whatever can be done with it?' But he recovered quickly. Humanity, with all its imbecilities and weaknesses, was all there was to bring into being the great gods' decrees. He held up his left forefinger and pointed. 'Fionn, carry him down – with care – to my workplace. I will do what must be done.'

'No better man,' thought Fionn as he gave quick orders for that to be done. A cloth was brought, the body transferred to it, and the limp burden carried round the path beneath the ramparts of Tara, to the main gate and from there down the hill to Taoscán's cave.

Only at the gate did Cormac make an appearance, Prince Cairbre by his side. He pointed to the sorry figure being carried by the four men. 'What happened him? Or who is he?' Cormac asked.

'Siascán, Your Highness.' And Fionn quickly told as much as he, or any of them, knew.

Cormac's face darkened as he listened. 'I knew it! I knew we should have acted at once when that . . . dirty thing . . . was nailed to my gate. But there'll be steps taken now, that much I promise.' He whipped round on Fionn, but on Taoscán too, his finger stabbing. 'I want . . . action! Today! No more delay. Or else they'll think they can attack us in our very beds!'

Fionn looked blankly towards the western horizon,

wishing he were out there hunting stag or wild boar together with Bran and Sceolaing – even wrestling with wolves – rather than here listening to a man who spent most of his life in bed anyway. But he knew – his grandfather, Tréanmhór, had told him so often enough – that one must listen to thunder. So he stood there, yet only half-hearing. For he recognised all too well himself now that the time for action had come. Cormac was correct in that at least. If something decisive was not done now, worse was sure to follow. But what should be done?

Only Taoscán could provide a sensible answer to that.

Just after noon, the guard Fionn had left at Taoscán's door to inform them of developments rushed breathless into the courtyard. 'He wants you below, Fionn. Now!'

'Right,' said Fionn. 'An' you'd better tell His Highness too – after you have something to quench that terrible thirst I see in your face that's nearly stopping you from talking.'

He grinned slyly, winked, and the messenger grasped his throat, nodded, and staggered in a wide circle towards the vat of cold water that stood at the furthest reach of the yard, under the catwalk just outside the door to the banqueting hall.

Fionn made no delay in arriving at Taoscán's door. And this time there were no formalities, except what the body of Siascán – covered now – demanded.

'It is exactly as I feared,' Taoscán began, without even looking at Fionn. 'This . . . thing . . . ' – he pointed to where the brain-ball lay in pieces on a smooth slab – 'came from the very same place as those on the gate. The same proportions of *dób buí* and *dób dearg*. Mixed by the same hand.' He slumped down, just as hurried footsteps – many of them – drew closer outside. 'You know what this means, Fionn, don't you?'

And Fionn had only time to nod sadly before a furious hammering began on the door.

'Open it,' sighed Taoscán. 'If they want the worst, then they must have it.'

Fionn did so, and in trooped Cormac, Cairbre and several of the Fianna. Cormac spoke at once. 'Taoscán, let there be no more beating about the bush. I want answers – now, this minute.'

Fionn could not help but note the fluster on the one side, dignity on the other, and not for the first (or hundredth) time he knew who the High King of Ireland should really be. But he held his peace. There was no profit in such observations now. Instead he stood, arms folded, alert, and listened.

'Answers are easy,' said Taoscán. 'It is the correct questions we must be careful to ask.'

'Well, I'm asking this one question now, an' I want an answer straight away: who's behind these . . . these outrages? Tell me that or nothing!'

'I can tell you that all right. The man who made these' – he pointed to the fragments on the slab – 'was Dubhdraoi, a colleague of mine for a while once. But why he did it is harder to answer. Men's motives take many shapes, as well you know yourself. Let us put final blame on no one – yet.'

Fionn thought for a moment that Cormac might reach out, snatch at Taoscán and shake him. But no. He seemed to shrink slowly as his temper subsided, and at last he said lamely, 'Tell us, so, an' what we need to do will be done.'

'Sit,' said Taoscán, and he made it sound so much like an invitation that not one of those present could refuse. As they each fumbled to find a place, he began: 'Yes, it is from the shore of Loch Neacach these ugly things have come. The meeting place of the south and east shores – a corner called Aill Bhuí. Between Ard Mór and Doire Fhada.'

'I often hunted boar in that very wood,' cried Fionn.

'Whose land is that place in?' interrupted Cormac rudely.

'That I leave to other heads,' answered Taoscán evenly. 'What concerns me now is to make certain that there is an end of this lowness, this villainy.' He turned to Fionn. 'The dangerous task falls on yourself and the Fianna – as you would wish, I think.'

'That's our job,' smiled Fionn. 'An' there'll be no shortage o' volunteers, that I'm sure of. The men have had enough o' the quiet life here at Tara for a while. A bit o' danger'll do 'em no harm at all.'

'Ah, but it is the *kind* of danger that matters, Fionn. And to make sure you have more protection than mere steel can provide, call here to me before you set out.'

'An' that'll be tomorrow morning at first light,' Cormac announced.

Fionn nodded, bowed himself out, his men with him, leaving Cormac and Cairbre to sort out details with Taoscán. He had much work to do if that was how soon they must be on the road north to Uladh, Loch Neacach and . . . who knew what!

At cockcrow a trumpet blast shivered the silence over the hill. Mutters, creaking beds, growls, curses, then gasps as cold water met warm faces and shoulders. All the normal sounds of an action-day.

Diarmaid could have laughed as he strode down between the bunks snapping out orders: 'Come on, Goll, is your backside stuck to the bed, or what? Out of it, Oscar, you lazy animal!' And as he whipped the horsehair quilt from Caoilte, rolling him out on the floor with a thump, he shouted, 'Get up, there, Caoilte, or we'll leave you here after us on the floor, dreaming of your fast races an' quick escapes from danger. Heh, heh!'

There was no malice either in his roughness or the 'Go 'way, you evil beast!' that greeted him from every corner. It was standard practice – the same on every cold morning at this time of year. Hated, yet welcomed.

After breakfast, and when those who were going north (it was only with difficulty that a garrison had been persuaded to remain at Tara) were assembled before Taoscán's cave, there was a surprising development. For not alone did Taoscán step out to address them, and Fionn too – they expected that – but there also stood Cairbre.

He was stared at by the four ranks of hard, grim warriors, and many of them groaned silently. He was not known as a forthcoming lad, or even as one who carried weapons in public. Reading, yes. Poetry, yes. History too. That was fine, but not now. They hoped he was not coming with them. The last thing they needed on a mission like this was babysitting the High King's son. For if anything happened him . . . ! One mission at one time was enough. Yet they stood at attention and waited for Fionn or Taoscán to speak.

It was Fionn who did so, and briefly too. 'Listen to Taoscán, men. He'll tell ye more than I can.'

No one moved an eyelash. They were accustomed to lunatic addresses from Cormac. What Taoscán, in his calm voice, would have to tell them was at least bound to make sense. And it did.

'You have all seen the doings of the past few days here at Tara. They have been ugly. And part of the blame must fall on me. For it is I who most hate these brain-balls: not for the bodily deaths they cause, but – as I have explained to Fionn – for what they do to the spirits of the dead in the next life. If nothing is done now, all of us are in danger, as you see in the case of Siascán. Only one thing will suffice. The maker of these hateful things must be sought out and brought here to Tara to account for his deeds. And where they are made must be destroyed.' He paused at that, then walked the length of the front rank, and back. 'If you can do that much, men, then I, as far as my power can stretch, will protect your going and coming.'

They listened, each one of them. Fionn could see that. And so that no one might be in any doubt about the consequences of this course of action, Fionn added: 'There will be danger on this journey, make no mistake about that. Death too, maybe. But if any man here is afraid o' danger or death, let him fall out now, an' there'll be no dishonour to him, I promise it.'

No one stirred.

'Good. I expected no less. One hour. Be ready to go. We're on a mission here that's for the honour o' the Fianna an' the safety of Ireland.'

All forty of those who had been chosen (amid bitter protests from those who had not) trooped to the main gate, fully equipped, exactly an hour later. Taoscán was waiting there, obviously with something further to say. They grew silent, expecting another speech. But what they got was far more practical: a druidic blessing, in language so ancient that not one of them could understand a word of it.

'That's the stuff!' whispered Diarmaid to Caoilte. 'It must be powerful if we don't know what he's saying.'

And when it was finished, Taoscán repeated almost the same sentiment: 'Now, at least, whatever befalls you, I will know of it. But still, as well you know, I will not dishonour anyone among you by easy saving from what must be faced by each of you. Only if the worst becomes the worst will I intervene.' And they were more than content with that.

But there was one other small matter, and completely unexpected, too. Just as they were turning to go, Cormac and Cairbre stepped out the gate. 'Take good care o' this lad, Fionn,' the High King said. 'If anything happens to him, I'll hold you responsible.'

'But . . . but . . . '

Cormac, though, had already turned and was strolling back inside, as if he had just done the most normal thing in the world.

Fionn swung around to Taoscán, about to break into a streel of complaint. But his old friend already had his forefinger to his lips. 'Shh! I have taken account of this. The boy will be of use to you, make no mistake of that.'

Fionn growled, turned on his heel and gave the order to move, motioning Cairbre to fall in with the rest. He was annoyed, but if Taoscán thought it was . . . oh, to hell with it! He was not to blame if Cormac had so little regard for his eldest son.

'But if he thinks he'll get special treatment,' he muttered, 'he has another think coming.'

As they marched off on the northern highway, the many men on the battlements watched them glumly.

'Some people have all the luck,' snarled Dlúthach, almost in tears at the prospect of bloodshed missed, and a hundred heads nodded mournfully.

There was nothing to hinder the Fianna as they passed through the rich lands of Meath and on north-east towards the Boyne and the ford of Breó at Ros na Rí. Workers in the fields straightened as they passed.

'There must be another war coming, or something,' was their usual observation before they bent again to their labours. War or no war, their routine would change little. Moving at a leisurely pace, the warriors arrived at the ford in little over an hour and a half, and before wading respectfully through its sacred waters (they could have jumped across if they had wished but preferred its cooling blessing), Fionn called a brief halt to admire the view. 'I can never pass here without feeling a kind of . . . '

'Reverence?' asked Diarmaid.

'The very word. But something else, too. A sort of . . . fear. There's thousands o' years o' the gods' presence in this place. Look over there to the left, the House o' Cleíteach. A pity Cormac doesn't use it like the kings at Tara did once. An' on the far bank up the river there – that's Sídh Chnoghbha. Look down there to the right, then an' ye can see Sídh Breasail at Dubhat. I tell you, they're places to be kept away from on Lá Bealtaine or at Samhain. Oh, I could tell ye stories about them two places.'

'Do! Do!' they pleaded, gathering round him, as if they were in the banqueting hall back at Tara.

'Here? Are ye forgetting what we're about?'

But as they pulled back, a little shamefaced, he added: 'When we get back here after finishing our business at Loch Neacach, I'll tell ye. An' ye won't be disappointed, either. But now there's one other thing I have to warn ye about – though I'm sure ye have it all heard before. When we're passing just to the left o' that huge mound straight over across the river there – Sídh i mBroga – let there be no word spoken, no matter what ye may see or hear. That's the most dangerous of 'em all. That's where Taoscán says the Dagda lives, an' if he says it, I believe it. Why this road was built next to it, I'll never understand. But it was. An' the sooner we're beyond it, the better for all of us. So come on, an' not a sound until I give the signal.'

They crossed then, and passed by that entrance to the other world silently, almost on tiptoe, with many a cautious sideways glance at the dark opening behind its strangely carved stone. And even when Fionn, over a mile further on, said, 'Talk away now as much as ye like', there were few who responded. Each man, he noted too, had a tight grip on sword- or dagger-hilt.

'You'd think they'd know by now how little use our weapons are against the other world,' he thought, but he said nothing. Better to keep up a good pace and hold in mind what might lie ahead. They would need all their skills (and Taoscán's help too) for that.

Hardly an hour later, they came to another ford, at Sliabh Bregha, and it was there that Fionn told them to rest awhile and have a drink – and a fish, if they could catch any!

While the men sat and chatted, he took Diarmaid aside. 'We're making good progress, an' if we can keep it up we should be able to get to Lios Liath, just beyond Sliabh Gullion, by the fall o' night. If we do that, we'll make camp there. You can be sure that as we get nearer to where we're going, there'll be eyes watching out for us. We'll have plenty time in the morning to make our plans for getting as near to Loch Neacach as we can unnoticed.'

'If we last through the night!' laughed Diarmaid.

'None o' that kind o' talk!' Fionn was not smiling. 'It'll be one of our biggest problems, lasting through tonight. These are no ordinary enemies we're up against here. But Taoscán told us he'll be helping us all he can. The rest we must do ourselves.'

'But why not use Sliabh Gullion itself? We'd nearly be able to see Loch Neacach from the top of it.'

'Too open. An' too big to defend. The place I have in mind is handier. You'll see.'

He stood, then gave the order to march again, and they continued on northwards, keeping as much as possible to the west of the kingdom of Airghialla. The last thing they needed on this mission was a local squabble with some lord who felt they were an invasion force from Tara.

And the few groups of natives they met on that day's journey were by and large friendly. Some of them even recognised Fionn, especially among the Fir Rois, for whom he had done favours several times on previous hunting expeditions. They offered food, shelter and entertainment for the night, but Fionn declined politely.

'But on our way back from this business of ours, maybe we'll take up that kind offer,' Fionn told them. 'We appreciate it, no matter what, an' Taoscán Mac Liath will hear of it.'

They were satisfied with that, and the Fianna continued towards Lios Liath.

'There's times when hospitality is nearly as bad as hostility,' Fionn laughed, but Diarmaid could see that he was pleased, all the same, to be recognised and welcomed.

Dusk was well advanced when they finally came to the place Fionn had in mind for their overnight camp. It was a low hill with large boulders scattered about its sides, a grove of spindly firs decorating its summit.

'You picked a lonesome enough spot, Fionn,' declared Goll. And just then, against the fading sun, it looked anything but welcoming or comfortable.

'It'll give us some protection, at least. There isn't a better place I know of within another hour's march o' here.'

'But why has it a name like Lios Liath, when there's no fort here?'

'There was,' replied Fionn shortly. 'One time. It was burned.'

He volunteered no more information, so they began immediately, shifting boulders into even better positions, filling the gaps between them with tree-trunks and rubble to chest height.

When that had been done to Fionn's satisfaction they sat in a ragged circle, opened their travelling satchels and began to eat. And not without complaint, of course, about how the food had been mushed and mashed during the journey. But it was welcome, for all that, because apart from the water at Sliabh Bregha, they had had nothing since early morning. Then, without much more delay, it was time for sleep.

'Múchán, take first watch,' Fionn ordered. 'Conán, be ready to back him up. Only wake the rest of us if ye have to.'

They rolled themselves into their cloaks then, and Múchán leaned on his spear and watched. Indeed, there was little to be seen in the dark, for no fire had been lit. 'No point in showing 'em where we are,' Fionn had said. 'I'm full sure they'll find us anyway if they want us.'

He was correct in that much, for within an hour, just as a drizzle began to drift down on the hill, making Múchán shiver, a figure was creeping towards them, dark of dress and evil of intent.

The first hint Múchán had of this presence came as he straightened numbly once again from his cramped and painful left leg. 'Owph!' he breathed and tumbled sideways.

It was the saving of his life, for at that instant something hard – something with his death wished into it – whistled by his ear and struck one of the trees behind him with a dull 'Pthukh!'

As Múchán staggered for balance, a rasping sound on the nearest boulder made him freeze. Shading his head behind the crook of his arm – for he had laid his helmet aside – he sank to one knee and scrabbled with his left hand for his spear, found it, inched it towards him. He could hear his own breathing, but nothing else.

'Whoever this is, 'tisn't his first murder in the dark,'

Múchán reflected, his confidence beginning to come to him. 'The one that makes the next sound is the dead one.'

Neither of them did, in fact. It was the arrival of Goll, visited by exploring insects of some kind, who squirmed in his cloak, muttering obscenities and scratching violently, that provided the chance Múchán needed.

Múchán kept his eyes trained on the boulder where the noise had sounded, and suddenly he saw it: a light blur in the dark, as of a hand raised. He sprang up, flung his spear and 'Thunnk!' it connected with flesh – and bone, too.

'Up! Up, quick!' he yelled. 'We're attacked.'

In seconds swords, spears were bristling in every direction.

'Where?' shouted Fionn. 'Who's on guard?'

'Me,' hissed Múchán. 'But listen.'

An immediate hush, and they heard it. And there was no mistaking it, either: 'Ghhh-aaa-khhh!' A death-rattle.

A torch was speedily lit, then shaded, and Múchán and all of them saw what had been done. A man was lying there, his eyes staring, blood trickling from the left corner of his mouth into his beard. His features were dark. In fact, everything about him seemed dark, including his cloak.

They stood there silently until Fionn hissed harshly, 'To your posts. Take shelter. Be ready. There may be others.'

By the light of the torch, he and Diarmaid examined the dying man closer. He could have been any assassin. Except perhaps for one thing: a small black medallion on a short dark chain around his neck.

'Ah!' breathed Fionn, pointing to it. 'D'you see what I see, Diarmaid?'

'I do. But . . . what is it?'

'Look nearer. Tell me what you think is on it.'

Diarmaid squinted closer. 'Some sort of a serpent. An' another one twined up with him into a kind of a knot.'

'Exactly. An' the last time I saw that design, 'twas in the very same situation as this – intended murder in the dark. Did I ever tell you about it, about a character called Tnúthán?'

'You mentioned him, but that's all.'

'I'll tell you some time – if villainy, treachery an' murder are to your liking. But now . . . ' He leaned forward, twisted the necklace from the dying man's neck, pocketed it. 'This might be useful evidence later on, either for ourselves or for Taoscán.'

There was no more sleep that night. They all wanted to hear and hear again the details of what had happened. And at dawn everyone was most anxious to see for himself Múchán's handiwork.

Conán summed it up: 'All that target practice in the dark wasn't wasted after all.' And there was much nodding of heads. Once again, it had been shown that there was method in Fionn's madness.

'We'll bury him. We can't leave him for the wolves, though that's what he might deserve,' said Fionn. Then he turned to a matter that was maybe more important. 'Now,' he asked Múchán, 'where again did this thing you heard go?'

'It hit something behind me . . . over there.' He pointed – straight at the trees.

It took moments only to find the thing that had almost cost him his life, and as Fionn looked at it, then felt it, he smiled. 'You're a fortunate man to be able to see the sun today, Múchán.'

There, sunk a finger's length into the trunk of the tree, was a brain-ball, still in one piece.

'Whoever made that knew his job,' whistled Feardorcha.

'Lucky that the one he gave it to didn't know his job as well.' Múchán shuddered, but smiled.

Fionn, with his dagger, gouged it out, examined it. 'A pity I don't know as much as Taoscán about these things, but I'll wager it came from the same place as the rest.' He faced them all then. 'It tells us one thing clearly, though. They know we're on our way, so there isn't much point in trying to stay hidden from here on. *An módh díreach* – the direct attack, an' the fastest – is probably the best way to approach 'em now. Has anyone any different idea?'

'Whatever we have to do, we better do it in the daylight. They'll be learning from their mistake here tonight.' It was Liagán who said it.

Fionn nodded, but made no comment.

By the time the dark one was buried, Fionn had decided on their strategy. 'From here to Loch Neacach, the straightest way, is no more than half a day's journey – less if we run. But there's no sense in arriving too tired to fight. What we'll do is this. Diarmaid'll take half o' ye. The rest will come with me, including Cairbre. We'll go around an' approach from the west, an' Diarmaid, ye'll keep a straight line an' come on 'em from this side. Ye should have no trouble. 'Tis directly north from here, as straight as an arrow.'

No one disagreed with that, and when Diarmaid and his nineteen men had been given directions and told of landmarks, they prepared to part company.

'We'll meet at the western end o' the wood nearest the shore,' was Fionn's parting instruction. 'There's a lake there, surrounded by holly bushes. Ye can't miss it. An' if the worst of opposition comes to the worst, two blasts o' your hunting horn will tell us all about it an' where ye are. I'll do the very same if things go badly against us.'

And so they separated.

Whether their approach was being observed or not, there was no further attempt to interfere with their progress, and at mid-morning, close to Eamhain Macha, Fionn motioned his group to halt.

'We'll rest here for a short while an' look around us.' He pointed westward. 'There's Eamhain. If we weren't in a hurry, we could call an' say hello. An' I'm sure they'd have something on the table for us too. But we don't want to miss our meeting with Diarmaid.'

As they lay there on their cloaks, chewing grass-stems or scratching and spitting, they peered silently at the Hill of Eamhain, the great Tara of the north, and it occurred to more than one of them that the druids of that place should surely know of the making of the brain-balls so close to them. Or could that be another angle to the rivalry between Tara and Eamhain?

Fionn, for one, hoped not. 'I'd hate to think druids could sink to that kind o' thing,' he said to no one in particular.

But they all knew, of course, that such did happen.

Had not Garbhán disgraced his training?[1] And, come to think of it, weren't they, on this very trip itself, on their way to find whether Dubhdraoi, another of that august profession, was practising acts of darkness?

Fionn rolled over and sat up. Why was it always, he wondered, that when he began to consider rather than fight, the world took on a wholly more complicated appearance? 'I'll have to stop this oul' thinking,' he muttered.

'What's that?' Liagán asked.

'Oh . . . nothing at all. I was only talking to myself.'

'Is it that we're not good enough company?' Liagán teased, but when Fionn eyed him greyly and said nothing, he decided to let the matter drop. There were more immediate concerns to hand.

Fionn beckoned the men close to him. 'We'll go from here to the Abha Mhór. After that, all we have to do is follow it an' it'll take us to Loch Neacach.'

That made sense, and the rest of their journey was made even easier by Feardorcha's suggestion, on the river bank, that they should cut down a tree, clean off the branches and use it as a kind of boat.

'Good thinking,' Fionn said. 'The river is wide an' deep enough from here on to get us there. But be careful not to damage any oak, or Taoscán'll never let us hear the end of it.'

They needed no such reminding. Well they knew the specialness of oaks. The solution to their problem was even better: a huge ash that had recently fallen.

In ten minutes this tree had been separated from its curled and broken roots, the branches and top lopped off, and had then been manhandled the short distance to the water.

'Gently, now. As little noise as possible,' Fionn cautioned. 'We won't make it any easier for 'em to hear us than we have to.'

But as it was pushed forward into a still, dark pool, a fleeting thought occurred to him: 'Maybe 'tis they're making it easy for us.'

This thought niggled him enough for him to say, though laughingly, 'Be careful underneath ye. You'd never know what might be down there that'd eat the legs off of us.'

'Yerra, stop your oul' nonsense, Fionn. D'you think you're going to frighten us!'

'You're listening to too many monster stories.'

'Uuu! I think I can feel one of 'em at my toes already!'

'If he is, he won't be in it for long. Sure this is the first time your feet met water since you got married – an' what age are your grandchildren now?'

And on it went as they rode the log mile after mile downstream, using their swords to steer and row.

Only Cairbre, the serious observer, did not join the fun. He sat silent at the back, thinking of what Fionn had said. Every so often, unnoticed, he would lift one leg, then the other, out of the water to make sure nothing was amiss. And as they came nearer the lake and the current slowed, he took to sitting cross-legged on the log. If he had been asked why, he would have been able to give no sensible explanation. It was just . . . a feeling he had that all was not as it should be.

And he was right, for as they floated into a wide, still pool, overhung with huge beeches which reached grey arms out towards each other from either bank, there was a sudden hush. Everyone stopped talking together, as if waiting for something to happen, though the surroundings were beautiful, albeit bleak.

'I wonder has this place a name?' asked Feardorcha, more to break the silence than to get an answer.

'If it hasn't, it should have.'

(It had, in fact. To locals it was Linn na bPúcaí, and it was avoided by all who knew it, every bit as much in daytime as at night. And the sailors found out why a moment later.)

'I must come back here sometime to fish – '

The words were hardly out of Liagán's mouth when the log gave a violent spin, throwing the rowers into the water. There was splashing and thrashing, of course, but only one, Cairbre, surfaced. He shook water from himself, gasped, spluttered, and then – noticed that he was alone.

'Fionn!' he shouted. 'Liagán! Oscar!' He jerked this way and that, confused, treading water. And then he saw – a row of heaving, squirming feet, pair after pair, tied together around the log, churning the water in a frenzy. He grasped his dagger, sliced through the thong tying the first, the second, the third, the fourth . . . and on down along the log, fright lending speed, precision to his progress. And behind him, body after body surfaced in a welter of foam, panting and gasping in of air.

Yet even Cairbre, despite his best efforts, could do only so much. One thong in particular, three from the end, defied him, and as he sawed grimly, he cursed the cow whose hide it came from, seed, breed and generation. He should have left it and cut the other two. Of course he should. But who can be wise at such a time?

When finally it snapped, the last two pairs of feet had ceased moving, and though he freed them there and then, there was no scrabbling for air, no arms snatching upwards. He watched, horrified, as one body, then the other, floated slowly to the surface.

It was Fionn who elbowed him roughly out of the way, grasped the two and rolled them over in the water. In spite of his own narrow escape, his first thought, as always, was for his men. 'Get 'em out o' here, quick!'

Within moments, both of them, as well as the owner of the tough rawhide, were on the bank, but he at least was able to do his own coughing. But the other two – now recognisable as Daolghus and Múchán – no matter how much they were squeezed, thumped and breathed into, made no move.

There was only one thing to do now, and Fionn did it. His left hand stabbed towards his magic oxter-bag, fingers struggled to loosen the thong that held it closed (and watertight, he hoped!), every face there urging him on – 'Open it! Open it!' – especially those two pale, lifeless-looking ones. Near-panic lent him strength. Thumb and forefinger poked down deep into the bag's magic darkness, then outward. Only it could help him now.

But nothing met his touch! He pushed deeper. Still nothing. This had never happened before in all the times he had been forced to seek the oxter-bag's aid. He jerked out his hand, confused. But no sooner came his fingers to sight than he was almost knocked by the stench from them. Rotting bodies would have been as perfume compared to it. He staggered, nearly vomited, as he turned away. And all the others stumbled back in disarray, coughing.

But then – a little thought! Coughing? Maybe that was it. Fionn, in two steps, was kneeling by Daolghus's head, those stinking fingers held inches from his nose. 'Come on! Come on!' he muttered impatiently, his teeth clenched.

And sure enough, a nostril twitched. Then Daolghus's eyes sprang open, stared an instant in shock at nothing. He leaped up then with a shriek: 'Aaa-iii! They're after me! Save me!'

But Fionn was already at work on Múchán, almost poking his fingers up his nose. But this time . . . there was no response, though he kept at it for a full fifteen minutes. When he finally rose, slowly, hunched, no one spoke for a few moments.

It was Liagán who broke the silence at last. 'Fionn, you did what you could – *more* than anyone could. If the oxter-bag couldn't bring him back, nothing in this world could.'

Fionn only rubbed his brow, stood as if puzzled. 'But what was Taoscán doing? He said he'd be watching over us.'

Liagán squeezed Fionn's shoulder. 'You know what the same man told us often enough, Fionn: "No man lives beyond his day." Múchcán's time was up, that's all.'

Fionn nodded. 'Maybe. But I can promise you this much. This day's work won't go unpaid for. That I swear. An' I don't care who's against us, or what power he has.'

'That's the way I like to hear you talk,' Liagán said, with a smile. 'Just remember that an' all the rest of us might see Tara again safe.'

'I will. Have no fear o' that.'

Liagán had none. In fact, he sympathised in advance

with Dubhdraoi – if he was the one responsible, that is.

There was a few minutes' discussion about what should be done next. Should they carry the body with them?

'No. It'd only slow us. An' this crowd we're up against will stop at nothing, now that they have this much done.'

Guard the body there?

'No. Too dangerous. This is their ground. They know every inch of it.'

Take him back to Tara?

It took no great argument to decide that this was probably the best option. It would avoid possible dishonour to the dead, and the four bearers, when they arrived at Tara, could tell of the ugly deed and see what the reaction would be, especially Taoscán's.

Fionn was delighted to find, though, that there were no volunteers to leave. Every man there wanted to go on, no matter what the risk, and only when lots were finally drawn did the four who were chosen agree to go back.

Diarmaid and his group, in the meantime, were having problems of their own, none of them major in itself, but each one in its way ominous.

The first occurred at the northern end of Loch Cam, hardly twenty minutes after they had parted company with Fionn and the others. They found their way blocked by a particularly dense belt of stunted trees. Their options were either to keep travelling west until they found a break, or swim around it, or hack their way through. There seemed only more of the same westward, and none of them felt like facing freezing water, so they hacked.

But as they did so, their hair and clothes were continually dragged and pulled by thorns as sharp and clinging as briars. Only when they had forced a path through and were resting a moment did Goll turn, an odd look on his face. He looked at his companions, then back at what they had just struggled through. 'Am I losing my wits, or . . .?' He rose and began to examine the cut branches.

'What's at you?' Conán asked him. 'Sit down, can't you, an' rest while you're able.'

Goll continued, as if he had not heard, then held up one of the same branches. 'Tell me, what kind of a tree is that?'

'Beech, o' course,' came the reply, without hesitation.

'Yes, indeed. But when did any one o' ye ever see beech with thorns on it?'

They gathered closer. There was no denying it. And the same all the way back through the thicket.

'I think,' said Diarmaid at last, 'that someone is trying to delay us, an' I think I know the reason.'

'I can guess who, an' why, too,' growled Aedh.

Diarmaid nodded. 'Come on,' he said. 'The sooner we meet Fionn again, the better I'll like it.'

They readied themselves, and trooped on. But hardly ten miles further north, while crossing a little river, they were startled – and dismayed too – when one (the middle) of three stepping stones that Conán had just jumped onto made a sudden dart upstream, throwing that rough warrior flat on his back into the water.

There were laughs and cheers, of course, as he struggled up, until men saw what had, in fact, happened. The jesting died away as he stood there, water to his knees, gaping at the stone, which was now fixed where it had stopped, several feet from the other two.

He looked helplessly around a moment, then: 'Is it so I'm . . . dreaming . . . by any chance . . . ?'

They were all looking at, and all seeing, the same thing. No one could doubt that.

Diarmaid was the first to gather courage to approach the stone. Carefully, from a few feet away, he poked it with his spear. But it was fixed as firmly as if it had been there for centuries. He shrugged, mystified. And none of them could put the fall down to a misstep by Conán. The stone was upstream from where it had been.

'But why didn't it move when the five men ahead o' you stepped on it?' his brother asked.

Conán shook his head. 'Maybe there's someone trying to tell me something.'

'I think you might be right,' muttered Diarmaid. 'But come on, we'll keep going. The more they try to frighten us, the more they must be afraid o' meeting us.'

But the omens were not ended yet. For, almost two hours later, as they rested briefly before crossing the River Bann and Diarmaid was encouraging them – 'We'll be meeting Fionn an' the lads in a lot less than an hour's time' – a strange barking howl close at hand cut in on his words.

He stopped, taken aback by it. All of them were. 'What in the name o' the seven sages is that?' whispered Céadach.

No one replied, for there it was again, a cackling wail, as if they were being mocked and mourned all at the same time.

'It must be the banshee,' breathed Mac Lughach.

But he was wrong, as they saw a moment later, when a white blackbird – they recognised it by its bill – skimmed past them and perched on an oak branch nearby. No one moved. It leaned out, facing them defiantly, and began its horrible noise again.

'He's talking to us, no doubt o' that,' said Diarmaid.

'Will I shut him up?' growled Conán. 'A knife between the eyes – that'd make him sing a different song.'

'No such thing,' snapped Diarmaid. 'D'you see the tree he's on? If you missed, an' hit that . . . !'

'I'll give him something else so,' smiled Conán.

'What?' Diarmaid asked, suspicious.

'This' – and he leaped forward with a yell – 'Yee-haaaa!' – that shook the very ground under them.

The bird stood a moment, petrified, its eyes two black balls in its head, then slid slowly sideways and down, its claws frozen, clinging to the branch. There it hung upside down, senseless as Conán approached.

'Heh, heh! He won't annoy people with that racket again for a while.'

No one answered him. They had all been frightened nearly as much as the bird.

'Hmm,' glowered Diarmaid at last. 'I'm inclined to think that that mightn't have been the best way o' doing things.'

'How d'you mean? Didn't I get rid o' that horrible noise!'

'You did. But the horrible noise you made means they'll know for sure we're coming.'

'An' if they do, itself, what about it?' he replied, becoming indignant. 'Are we afraid of a gang o' murderers in the night – low types that won't even face us in the daylight?'

'That may be, but – '

A severe argument might have begun there and then – one that could have been no assistance to any of them –

had not, at that instant, two long blasts of a hunting horn sounded from somewhere to the north-west. Every movement ceased. They listened intently.

'We're forgetting ourselves,' said Diarmaid hurriedly. 'Come on! Out o' here, quick.'

And they did. At double-pace, too, they went. But not before the white bird had been snatched from his branch and pocketed by Conán . . . just in case! And there were no more distractions – or if there were they went unnoticed, for Fionn's instructions were again clear in all of their minds: the hunting horn's sound meant trouble.

As it happened, when the two groups met almost an hour later, exactly where they had arranged, Fionn's band seemed in no serious difficulty, though they looked downcast.

'Why'd you sound the trumpet, Fionn?' Diarmaid demanded, annoyed.

'I chewed my thumb o' knowledge by accident when I was eating a hazelnut I found on the path, an' I saw at once what was happening to ye. It might have got worse – to no one's profit.'

Diarmaid nodded, shrugged. Then he noticed the absence of Múchán and the four others. 'Where is – ?'

He got no further. Fionn held up his hand. 'We'll tell ye about it, maybe, on the way home. But here is where our task lies now. Not a mile from where we stand, there's evil work afoot that we have to put an end to. And we will! So come on. This is it – what we came all this journey for.'

There was no arguing with those sentiments, so they

turned east, keeping the lake-shore all the while in sight.

'Isn't it the next best thing to an ocean!' Caoilte marvelled.

''Tis, but we'll have some other time for admiring it,' Fionn said gruffly. 'Keep a close watch on the shore. That's where we'll find what we're looking for, surely.'

They had gone only a short way when Doire Fhada began in earnest: beautiful oaks, ash, beech and holly stretching in some places to the very water's edge. They stopped a moment to consult on how best to proceed.

'Three groups,' said Fionn shortly. 'One on the left for the shore, one on the right for the wood, an' one in the middle to keep the two in touch.'

And thus they advanced cautiously, spears in hand, daggers and swords loosened for instant action. Yet all was peaceful and quiet as they moved forward. Even the lake, grey beyond its low, marshy shore-meadows, was silent.

'If the land here is all as low as this, Fionn, I don't know where they could be making brain-balls,' sighed Oscar. 'There's nothing here but rushes.'

'Ah, but wait. Not so far from here, you'll see something a bit different.'

And his memory was accurate, for no more than ten minutes later the ground began to rise suddenly into a rocky outcrop.

'By the Lord Lugh,' mused Feardomhain, 'this is a bit like the Burren. I bet there's a story about how this place came to be.'

'There is,' nodded Fionn, 'an' a good one. But that can wait for another time.'

He motioned those nearest him to the edge of the height overlooking the water. It was no more than thirty feet but seemed enormous in contrast with the flatness all about it. A forefinger to his lips, he beckoned them and the others farther off to the verge. 'Down!' he whispered. 'Don't be seen.' And they sank to their knees, then onto their bellies, crawled forward and peered.

What they saw below made them stare, and caused no little alarm too. For there at the foot of the little cliff on which they lay was a hive of activity, neatly hidden from prying eyes by a thick grove of bushes to east and west reaching to the lake's edge.

'Clever, clever,' whispered Fionn. 'But look at what they're doing.'

And it was there for all of them to see – or at least the part of it that was being done above ground. That there was more, unseen work going on was obvious from the scurrying below.

A kind of wall, in a half-circle, had been built from the shore the best part of a hundred paces out into the lake. From inside this, the water had been emptied, and there, exposed, was the yellowest *dób buí* any of them had ever seen. Men with wooden spades were digging it out of a hole that was already huge, while others shovelled it onto carts without wheels. These were lined up, being filled three at a time and drawn away by little mountain ponies, up the shore and . . . and out of sight of those watching above.

'There must be some kind of a cave down under us,' Fionn growled. 'An' you can be sure that's where the real work is being done. These lads here are only doing the slave labour.'

'It'd be no bother to put a finish to what we see here,' smiled Goll, his fingers twitching with impatience. 'Just break that wall out there, an' we could drown the whole lot of 'em.'

'I know that, but it wouldn't finish the lad who puts the brain-balls together. He's the dangerous one – the one I want to bring back to Tara to meet Taoscán. If we don't get him – or *them* – we're only wasting our time, an' a good man has died for nothing.'

Diarmaid glanced sharply at Fionn as he said this, but Fionn was addressing Goll, being diplomatic (it was safer not to fall out with any of Goll's tribe, the Clann Mórna). 'When we're finished in the cave, though,' Fionn said, 'you can have the pleasure o' flattening that wall yourself.'

Goll smiled, and Fionn knew there would be no further argument.

For a while longer they watched, hoping to see someone of authority, but there was no one higher than the two foremen (one wielding a whip) who were keeping the diggers and horse-handlers hard at it.

'We're only wasting time here,' said Conán. 'The sooner we get down there an' sort 'em out, the better.'

'But wait now,' Diarmaid cautioned. 'There must be some other entrance. Look at that place below. Does that look like somewhere they bring out the brain-balls that are finished? I don't see any sign of a road away from here. Or a trace of any boats.'

'True enough,' Fionn nodded. 'There must be another way. An' if we don't find it soon, darkness'll be on us, an' then we'll be like last night – at their mercy.'

'Maybe not, maybe not,' smiled Mac Méin. 'They'll be

expecting big monsters like ye. An' 'tis hard for big men to hide. They know that. But me, now . . . If I took Cnú Dearóil there with me, we could search the wood without being noticed, while ye stay here an' guard this door.'

Fionn thought quickly. Just because these two were the smallest of the Fianna did not mean they were any less brave or skilful than the rest. But they had been laughed at often enough because of their size. He knew that. So maybe this was their best chance on this mission to prove themselves on their own.

'All right,' he said slowly. 'Do that. Search for the other way out. But carefully, mind. No hasty attacking. No heroic deeds – unless they're forced on ye, o' course. If ye find any other entrance, only bring back word of it here an' ye'll be mentioned to King Cormac – an' even more important, to Taoscán.'

They bowed, delighted, and melted into Doire Fhada without a sound.

'Huh! All right if we don't have to rescue 'em – from a badger or something like that,' sneered Conán sulkily.

'If every man does what he's supposed to, no one'll have any reason to complain,' Fionn replied quietly. It was true what his father had told him about the Clann Mórna's begrudgery, but this was neither the time nor the place for an argument.

They waited silently while dusk started to creep in around them. Below, work went on without a pause, even when the first torches began to be lit.

'Begod, but they must have a powerful lot o' customers, if they work by night as well as by day.' This observation of Céadach's was shared by all, and they wondered at the work that provoked it.

'A bit like the druid o' Feakle's tooth shop,'[2] added Diarmaid sadly. 'Isn't it amazing how those working for evil give every hour of every day an' night at it? 'Tis one thing I could never understand.'

Nor could the others, obviously, for there was no reply.

Cnú Dearóil and Mac Méin, meanwhile, were about their own business among the trees. What they were looking for was some kind of path, some sign of human traffic. But they found none, even though, for little men, they covered a great deal of ground in fine detail.

At last, with darkness only a short time away, they had nearly given up hope and were on the point of going back to the cliff (if they could find it!) when Cnú was taken short. 'Look away,' he said sharply to Mac Méin. 'I have something serious to do. Nature is calling.'

His companion sidled in behind an oak trunk and the little man fumbled with the tyings of his trousers. But no sooner had he crouched to relieve himself than the ground under him moved, rose and tumbled him backward into a most undignified position.

His first thought was that it was a joke in very bad taste by Mac Méin. He was about to shout something abusive, but the sudden appearance of a light, a torch . . . from the very ground! . . . stopped him. He froze, forgetting his dignity. And just as well he did so, for a trapdoor covered by leaves had been thrown back and a head and shoulders had appeared from a hole in the earth, the torch held aloft. Mac Méin, behind the tree, saw at once what was there and hoped that Cnú would have the sense to stay still. It was his only hope of remaining undiscovered.

And he did. But as the holder of the torch rose further and at last stepped out on to solid ground, he fixed his attention on Cnú. 'Worthless dwarf, do you think we have so little respect for ourselves that we allow creatures like you to foul our doors of coming and going?'

As he said it, his hand was reaching inside his cloak – which was black, Mac Méin noted! Time to intervene, he decided. And quickly. 'Nothing as foul as yourself, ugly – '

The dark one whirled, his hand flashed back and in the same instant Mac Méin ducked behind the oak. Lucky for him he did, for he heard rather than saw what was meant for his head: 'Whshkk!' It struck the bark of the tree, glanced off, and whistled into the gloom, landing with a crackle among bushes some distance away.

And there would have been more of the same but for Cnú. He saw the dark cloak part again, knew that another brain-ball was on its way – no doubt for him – and leaped. Straight for the throat he went, grasped his man and felled him all in the one motion. Small he might be, but no less strong than any other member of the Fianna for all that. Once his fingers gripped a throat, only a direct order from Fionn could release them.

And so it was now. Like a terrier he hung on, while the man in black thrashed wildly, rolled and tried to break that iron grip. Not a single word did Cnú waste on him. Mac Méin was the one who did the talking – though it was more a chorus of encouragement: 'Good man. Break his neck! Squeeze the eyes out of him! Throttle him!' – all the while doing a delighted little dance.

But after a minute or two, when he saw the victim's face beginning to turn grey, his eyes writhing in his head, he had still enough wit to know that a dead enemy was of no use to them. 'Stop, Cnú! Don't kill him entirely.'

But the little man paid not the slightest heed, only squeezed on, enjoying every croak of his victim.

Options flashed through Mac Méin's mind: find Fionn to order the release? No good. The dark one would be the dead one by then. Try to pry those fingers loose? Pointless. No one's fingers were stronger than Cnú's. There was only one chance – a slim one – try to imitate Fionn's voice. A brief prayer, and he was on the point of opening his mouth when a crashing through the undergrowth behind them caused him to whip round. There – thank Lugh! (and probably Taoscán too) – was Fionn himself, with Caoilte and Diarmaid.

'What's happening here?' panted Fionn.

'Quick, Fionn! Tell him let go. Quick!' Mac Méin shouted.

'Release him, Cnú!' Fionn ordered.

Those three words saved the dark one's life. Diarmaid snatched up the torch and stepped between the little man and his victim, who lay sprawled now, hardly breathing.

Fionn patted Cnú's shoulder, then knelt to examine his handiwork. The first thing he noted was the neckband, the knotted snakes. He glanced at Diarmaid, nodding. 'Another one of 'em. We're near our destination, I think.'

'We might as well find out what we can from this lad, so – if we can get him to talk,' suggested Diarmaid.

'Shake him up there,' Fionn ordered. 'We haven't much time for gentleness now.'

That was tried. No response – which was hardly

surprising, for the deep hollows left by Cnú's fingers were still clearly visible.

'He'll be lucky if he ever talks again,' said Mac Méin, peering down over their shoulders.

'Well, there's only one hope, so,' added Fionn.

They knew what he meant: the oxter-bag again. The problem was, though, that never had it been known to provide the same answer twice to the same problem.

'Maybe Taoscán might put in a good word for us to Lugh an' his friends,' he shrugged. ''Tis now, if ever, we need that horrible stink to wake this lad.'

He stood and slowly dipped his fingers down under his oxter, into the bag. No one stirred while he rummaged, everyone fully attentive to see what wonder it might give forth this time.

As usual, it did not disappoint, though when Fionn drew out his hand there seemed at first to be nothing in or on it. He inspected it closely, front and back. Still nothing. 'Well, this is the first time ever the bag failed,' he whispered, disappointed. 'An' just when we needed it badly.'

But then – he could not say what tempted him to do it – he reached down, grasped the necklace as if to take it (Taoscán would need it as proof, maybe) . . . and at once all hell broke loose. The dark (seemingly dead) one sprang into a frenzy of kicking, bouncing and bucking, as if he were being attacked with red-hot needles. His eyes and mouth exploded open and his hands grasped his throat, as if he were trying to claw away some obstruction.

'Squeeze him! Hard! Quick, a couple o' ye!' Fionn shouted, and Diarmaid from the front and Caoilte from behind did that.

There was nothing for a moment, while they tightened their grip, but then a blast of air whooshed out of him and he seemed to fold and collapse like a punctured bladder. But he was up almost at once, breathing frantically now. In a short while, when he had calmed a little, he looked about him at the circle of warriors surrounding him. There was nowhere to go.

'Now,' said Fionn quietly, forgetting the necklace in the confusion, 'why don't you lead us to your master. He's a man we'd love to meet.'

The dark one merely glared at him, sucked in his cheeks, then spat directly into Fionn's face.

But if he expected a sudden outburst of rage, curses and action he was sorely disappointed, for Fionn never moved. Only his eyes changed, to that hard flinty greyness his foes had learned to fear – though in the gloom, that could not be seen now. When he spoke, his voice was cold, dangerous. 'I have tried to treat you honourably, but it is clear now that you have no understanding of that word. For men such as you, fear is all that matters. And so, sadly, fear it must be.' He nodded to Cnú. 'Finish what you began. And this time I won't interrupt. Start with his legs an' work upwards.'

He turned away then and said to the others, 'Block yeer ears. This will not be pleasant.'

Already, though, at the gleeful approach of his small tormentor, defiance was replaced by fear in the dark one's face – and voice, too. 'No! No! Keep him away from me! He'll kill me!'

'He will,' Fionn nodded calmly. 'An' most painfully, too. If you think your last experience was bad, you know very little about him.'

He and the three others began to walk away, while Cnú, grinning evilly, drew closer.

'Stop! Wait! I'll tell ye . . . anything ye want.'

'A sensible decision, I'd say,' Fionn agreed quietly. The time for fun and levity was over. Work now. What must be done must be done, with no more delay.

'Lead the way, so,' Fionn hissed. 'An' remember, your good friend is right here behind you. One wrong move, an' you know what'll happen.'

With a nervous licking of lips, the dark one pulled his cloak closely about him as if cold, and gestured towards the trapdoor. Fionn merely nodded, pointed to Cnú, smiled and beckoned him on.

Down they went, step after stone step, the five of them following their unwilling guide, daggers drawn. At the bottom, twenty-one steps down, it was dank and pitch-dark.

'Make sure, Cnú, he doesn't get away on us, or we are at their mercy,' Fionn whispered.

'Have no fear o' that. I have a grip of his trousers. One wrong move, an' he'll be without one o' his legs.'

They started forward along a tunnel now, which was barely high enough to let the three large men pass. They had to hunch themselves, squeeze their heads down into their shoulders – either that or gash themselves against the rocky roof.

Feeling their way along like this, each man's hand on the shoulder of the man before him, they made their way like miners, until at last – how long, it was difficult to tell – they saw a glow ahead. And the closer they approached it, the wider it seemed, though hardly more bright. And now there were noises, too, mostly muffled and indistinct, but very definitely there.

Now Fionn sensed the passage floor was rising gradually, and he wondered what this might mean, but in a few minutes he was enlightened, as were all of them. For, of a sudden, they emerged onto a balcony maybe ten paces wide. Before them, blocking their way, was a rail of dark shiny wood beautifully carved in an intricate pattern of knotted snakes, and beyond it a roof lit from below by flickering lights.

Cautiously they crept forward, Cnú's fingers firmly grasping the flesh of their guide. Any false move there and 'Dark Cloak' would never walk again.

At first they hesitated to raise their heads even over the top of the rail, only peered through the fretwork. What they saw – or partly saw – below them changed all that, though. So much so that one by one they rose, slowly, unconsciously, mouths open, gaping. Not since the druid of Feakle's terrible tooth shop had they seen anything like it – those of them who had been there then, that is.

Luckily for all of them, Fionn, experienced in all manner of places, people and strategy, was not overwhelmed. 'Keep a tight hold of your man, Cnú,' he whispered, 'an' take him back down the tunnel there. If he jumps up or gives us away, it'll make our task a lot more awkward, an' there'll be more blood spilled than I want this night.' Obviously he was not expecting to depart without casualties.

Cnú tightened his flesh-grip, nodded and smiled. It was a well-taken precaution, for if they were seen, a blood-fight there and then could not be avoided. Honour would not allow it.

As things fell out (and by a seeming accident, too) there was another surprise in store for them first. Cnú was leading his captive back into the tunnel, but just as they shuffled past him, Fionn thought he noticed in the dark one's eye a flicker of more than torchlight. A mere shade of a fragment it was, yet of something other than fear. Could it be pleading? Despair? It was gone, with its owner, almost before it could register. But then Fionn remembered something else: that dark necklace, the proof for Taoscán. He had forgotten to take it. Well, now was the moment. He reached out and, with one finger, plucked it from the prisoner's neck and flicked it into the palm of his hand.

At once the other stopped, in spite of Cnú's shoving, his head jerked round, and not only Fionn but the others too saw the change that had come over his face. Gone was that dogged, sulky darkness. In his eyes now was a look of sheer relief – delight that none could mistake, even in the dim light.

The man stepped forward, dragging the startled Cnú the two steps with him, and planted a kiss squarely on Fionn's hand. In an instant, daggers were at his throat, but they were not needed. What the man did was signal them to be quiet and to move back into the shade of the tunnel. Which they did, but with weapons still at the ready.

When they were out of any danger of being heard by those below, he said in that narrow place, in a quiet but excited voice, 'Fionn Mac Cumhail, how I have waited – how we have *all* waited – for someone to do what you have just done!'

'What have I done?' Fionn asked quietly, though he knew well enough.

'Broken the spell put on me by Dubhdraoi. And please, please, do it not only for me, but for all those who work in this cursed place.'

'All in good time. For now, tell us more,' hissed Diarmaid.

He shook his head, covered his face with his hands. 'Oh! The foul, horrible things we have been forced to do here!' He was almost in tears.

'We'll hear more about all that later,' answered Fionn, though not unkindly. 'For now, tell us more about what's down there inside.'

'See it for yourself. But remember, when you do what you must, try not to injure those working there too much. They are under enchantment. They don't either know where they are or what they're doing.'

Fionn nodded. 'But how'll we know Dubhdraoi?'

'He's the one in the corner, supervising all. You will not mistake him, never fear.'

Fionn nodded again, but a small doubt was beginning to creep into his mind. Why had Dubhdraoi not intervened yet? Surely he, a druid, must know they were here and what was happening. Could this man's sudden conversion be a trick to lure them to their destruction? Or was Taoscán being active in assisting them?

He had to trust that such was the case, and keep going. How could they retreat now, in any case? 'All right,' he decided. 'We'll go on. But is there any way down off that balcony except by jumping?'

'Yes. Stairs both to left and to right. Observe this time and you will see.' They did exactly that as soon as their heads re-emerged from the tunnel, and it was as he said.

And now that that precaution had been taken, and the facts checked, they stepped to the rail, and studied in silence the scene below. No more peeping, squinting. They looked, in line, wordless.

And such a sight!

The room was surely forty paces by thirty. No small place. At the far end was a large door – the entrance from the lake, no doubt. Dividing the floor-space from front to back were four long tables, each one a hive of activity. The one on the left was obviously the head table – at least, its full length was covered in those gruesome objects, and more and more were being continually passed in by bloody hands under a curtain covering an opening at the far corner. And not all human, either. Among them were occasional animal heads – pig, hound, and, yes, wolf-heads too! Down along that table they were rolled, turned, twisted, poked, stared at every inch of the way, then passed to the second table.

There they were examined once again, more and more minutely as they travelled back up towards the door, until about halfway along . . . razors awaited, and they were one after another shorn and shaved, until, by the end of that table, each was as clean as a skull.

The heads passed by the door then, on to the third table, in a smooth, uninterrupted motion, then travelled slowly back towards the silent watchers, this time their every motion being one of dishonour. For this third table was one of varied talents: at its head, wearing a blood-spattered leather apron, hulked a swarthy smith-like man holding a short, dangerous-looking hammer. With one sharp blow in front of the ear, he exploded the top off each skull that was pushed within his reach, then revealed its contents and shoved it on to the next expert, who scoured with a curved knife the brain from its sheltering bone, tossing the remains – skull, eyes, teeth, skin – from him to whatever side of the table took his fancy. Which one mattered not at all, for there were baskets and attendants enough, and in plenty, to cart these scraps away.

By the time the brains – grey, sad holders of men's (and animals') thoughts, feelings, fancies, loves – passed to the end of this third table, they were being examined no more, but met by other knife-men, butchers. And in their manner there was nothing of love, mercy or respect. Each wrinkled brain was chopped as a mushroom might be – four quick, expert movements, there an end – and pushed on . . . and on . . . and on.

The disgust of those above was held in check only by their breathless fascination. How could such be happening in the land of Ireland? Where men like Taoscán . . . and Mogh Ruith . . . and Fíodh Mac Neimhe had power to prevent it? It did not make sense. But . . . but . . . when had the ways of right and wrong, good and evil, ever made sense?

And yet they stared, for as the pieces of brain were transferred to the fourth and last table, there to meet them was the *dób buí* and the mixers, squeezers and rollers. This last table appeared not so cruel after the others – how could it be! But it was here that happened what Taoscán would be most interested in. For here was the end product of it all: the brain-balls themselves. At the near end they could see for the first time the *dób buí* waiting, and as the bits and pieces of brains came one by one to that point and were mixed there, passed on up, rolled and shaped, there could be no more doubt. Here was where all the evil work came together. And yet . . . yet . . . they stared. For the ugly, horrible process was still not finished. At the far end of this last table, just as at the first, was an opening, this one on the right, and a curtain which was constantly moving as tray after tray of brain-balls was passed out.

They blinked, amazed, disgusted.

'But where are they going, out that window?' snarled Feardomhain.

'Out to the ovens, of course,' spoke the dark one.

'What!' almost shouted Caoilte.

'Shhh!' warned Fionn, the man of calm common sense, as ever.

'There's a whole other place out there to the right,' said their new friend. 'How else did ye think the brain-balls could be hardened to be delivered? In the soft mush o' table four, is it?' They had no answer to that.

But one solid fact they now had to face was . . . the man in the corner, busy writing behind his dark wooden table. He was hardly likely to welcome them to the room below, never mind to what might lie in the one beyond that. But he was there. And very much within range of a keenly aimed dagger from the balcony.

Fionn motioned them down, then whispered as much. 'He's a druid, I know, an' I don't even like to *think* of offering violence to such a one. But look what he's doing. No one should be let continue to dishonour the reputation of every other druid like that for even one minute more.'

'Shouldn't we try to capture him an' take him back? Taoscán an' the others, they're better judges than us,' offered Oisín.

'I know that,' Fionn agreed, 'but we were sent here to finish this filthy work. An' we will, by one means or another.' He considered a moment. Then: 'Here's what we'll do. We'll give him a chance to surrender – only one! Draw daggers now, an' when I give the signal, rise quick, an' be ready to nail him to the wall if ye have to.' As he said this, he unhooked his short but deadly spear, the *Gath Dearg*. 'An' if all else fails,' he murmured regretfully, 'this will be our last resort.'

There was no need to say more, for they all knew the spear's power. Few were the times Fionn had had to – or would consent to – use it, but those times were the most urgent. The result had always been the same: instant death for those (yes, even more than one at a single throw) it was aimed at. For it seemed to have a life, a mind, of its own, defying all defences, inevitably deadly.

'Maybe Taoscán'll make it unnecessary,' Fionn said. 'He said he'd be with us. But if he can't be . . . well, we have this to fall back on.'

He rubbed the smooth shaft lovingly, though sadly. He did not want to call on its services. But then . . . those ugly scenes below! Yes, it would be used if necessary. It would *have* to be.

'All right,' he breathed. 'The fastest way down is out over the balcony, an' legs first onto the tables. Three men to every table. That'll make enough *ruaille buaille* below while the rest o' ye are taking the stairs. Goll, lead on the left side, Conán on the right.' He picked out silently the twelve he wanted, then jabbed his thumb towards the balcony. 'An' remember,' he said softly as he straightened to go, 'the lad at the table is mine.'

With that, he flicked his arm forward, and as one, the twelve, himself at their head, sprang onto the balcony-beam and crouched a moment, eyes darting here and there, like some flock of huge birds, before launching themselves on their prey below, knives clamped in their teeth.

In three waves they dropped, seconds apart, feet slamming onto the table-ends, sending shudders up the chamber. But Fionn had eyes for nothing – not the shocked faces, the confused leaping back, the skull-cracking hammer poised in mid-motion – nothing except his man.

He jumped from the third table to the fourth, galloped, clattered along it, sending *dób buí* as well as its mixers and shapers flying. Two more leaps, five seconds, and Dubhdraoi would be in his grasp.

But that was not to be – at least not yet. For Fionn, as he was about to spring, landed his left foot in a platter of brain-slices and slithered sideways, losing his balance and momentum. It was only for a moment, but enough to allow the druid time to rise and throw himself out the exit to his left.

In a gesture of fury, Fionn, though toppling, flung the *Gath Dearg*. It streaked to its mark, straight and deadly, but Dubhdraoi was already out, in a flurry of dark robe and grey cloak.

When Fionn stormed to the doorway, the *Gath* was stuck in the wooden jamb, still quivering. And pinned there was the grey cloak. But not its owner. He had thrown it off and was gone, into that next chamber.

Fionn approached the door cautiously, quickly surrounded by the others, then leaped in, knife up and ready.
In an eye-blink, he sized up what was there – a room as
big as the other, but so, so hot!

Workers aplenty. Ovens. Blazing hearths. Chimneys.
And a wide door at the opposite left corner: these he saw
too. He snatched his spear. 'Hold that cloak tight, Diarmaid.
Without it, he can't make himself invisible.'

He was already sprinting for the door as he said this.
But outside was a walled yard and, though he looked up,
down, left and right, there was no movement, no sound.

He returned to the oven-room, where the workers were
still standing, blinking, amazed. 'He's still in here somewhere,' Fionn rasped, his voice rising. 'I can sense it.' He
looked around as those bake-workers cowered, conscious
and frightened now, amid their ovens and trays of cooked
and ready-to-be-cooked brain-balls.

'Where is he?' Fionn roared, and they shivered, hands
twitching, shoulders crouched, as if they expected to be
whipped. 'Tell me where he is!' Fionn repeated, this time
more quietly, more dangerously. He fixed his withering
glare on an old man near him, and slowly began to reach
towards him as if he might pick him up and fling him. He
had no intention of it. In fact, he felt sorry for the fellow,
who was trembling now. But there was no other way. And
it had the effect that was needed. For without a word, the
man turned, and his eyes would have said all even if he
had not pointed . . . to the nearest of three huge hearths.

There was no fire in this one, for whatever reason, and
when Fionn leaped in onto the hearthstone and looked
up, he could see only darkness. Was it blocked? Yes. And

a moment later he realised why, when a trickle of soot and dust sprinkled about him.

'We know you're up there, Dubhdraoi. Come down now, or I'll have to do a thing I don't want to!' Fionn shouted up into the chimney, and he gripped the *Gath Dearg*, ready to launch it. 'All I can tell you is, you'll be hit in a place that'll hurt a lot.'

There was no smile as he said it, only a gesture to Diarmaid to go out immediately, find the smoke-hole above and prevent him from escaping that way.

That was done at once, and Fionn turned again to the chimney. 'My patience is nearly finished,' he said shortly. 'Come down *now*, or blame yourself for what happens.'

There was a rustle above, a sharp crack, then a scraping, as of fingernails along stone. 'Aaa-unkh!' With a thump, Dubhdraoi landed beside Fionn in a dishevelled heap, still clutching the iron pot-hanger to which he had been clinging. He looked anything except like a druid now as he half-sat there, dazed, sooty, looking up at the *Gath Dearg* inches from his face.

Fionn spoke down at him calmly. 'You're going back to Tara with us at the crack o' dawn. An' don't even think about spells or enchantment. It might succeed with us, but not with this lad' – he patted the *Gath*. 'He has a mind of his own. You'll be dead before you even know it.'

Dubhdraoi merely glared. He knew well enough that what Fionn said was all too true.

'Caoilte!' Fionn shouted then.

'Yes, I'm here,' the prince replied, pushing his way to the front.

'You're the man with the speed, Caoilte. As soon as it

dawns, hit the road for Tara an' tell what you saw here. Ask Taoscán to bring Mogh Ruith an' Fíodh Mac Neimhe to meet us if he can do it. If they came for the druid o' Feakle[3], surely this lad is every bit as bad.'

'I'll do that, never fear,' nodded Caoilte. 'In fact, I'll start out now if you like.'

Fionn considered a moment. 'No. Wait on. It might be extra trouble to watch this lad here until daylight, but I'll do that while the rest o' ye search this place inside out, take note of everything, guard the doors an' let no one escape.'

During the remaining hours of that evening and night, they did so, under Diarmaid's command, while Fionn performed the hardest job of all: never to take his eyes off Dubhdraoi. Not even once. To do so might have meant disaster. Many a time, as he heard the gasps of amazement or cries of disgust (once even the sound of vomiting – 'Someone needs a bit more training,' he thought, half-smiling), he was tempted to look away, but he never did.

And not once either did Dubhdraoi, sunk in his own thoughts, glance at Fionn. Was it shame? More likely fear, for the *Gath Dearg* was pointed at his head during all those hours.

In the first dimness of dawn, Caoilte began to limber up and loosen himself for what would surely be one of his most important journeys.

When he was ready to go, Fionn had but one instruction for him: 'Tell Taoscán we'll meet him either at Sliabh Gullion or else at Áth na mBreó. An' good luck go with you, safe an' fast.'

Caoilte nodded, turned and, still flexing his muscles, made his way outside.

Two minutes more and he was off, with a last, almost lazy, wave to those standing at the doorway. They watched until he disappeared into the trees, then they drifted back to whatever they had been doing.

'All we have to do now is wait here together like friends,' smiled Fionn grimly at Dubhdraoi. 'You, me an this,' and he patted the *Gath*. His companion was in no mood for smiles, though.

It had the makings of a long, dreary day, for Fionn especially, but there was no help for it. What must be done must be done. So it was with nothing short of amazement, half an hour later, that he heard the shout outside: 'Caoilte is back!' A moment later, Oisín tumbled into his presence and repeated the same: 'Fionn! You won't believe this, but – '

'That Caoilte is back? If he is, he shouldn't be.'

Despite this disturbance, he kept Dubhdraoi all the time in his sight, fearing a trick.

'No! Not that . . . but this!' Oisín said.

And there, impossibly, in the wide doorway, stood Taoscán, and not only he but also Mogh Ruith and Fíodh Mac Neimhe. Caoilte stood there too, humble, bringing up the rear.

'How . . . ?' Fionn, a man not easily amazed, *was* amazed. And his face showed it.

Caoilte shrugged, wiped his forehead, but there was a look of relief in his eyes. 'Down out o' the sky they came. Three birds. But I'll explain later,' was all he could say.

'No need of that,' smiled Taoscán. 'I was keeping a close eye on you, as I promised, Fionn, that's all. And if we got here a little bit early, I'm sure you won't mind.'

At the sound of his genial voice and as word spread, men began to crowd from all parts of both chambers and beyond, then pause as they saw the other two, his companions, distinguished also as druids by their grey cloaks. The workers, one after another, fell to their knees, heads bowed, expecting the worst for their late deeds. And for a little while they were left thus, while Dubhdraoi became the focus of all the newcomers' attention.

For a few moments, nothing was said. They merely stared, one side at the other, three pairs of eyes at one. Then Taoscán, always kind, sighed. 'First, let us put those unfortunates, his slaves, from under the spell he has laid on them. You agree?' he asked his two companions, quietly. They nodded.

Then with eyes closed, in an almost matter-of-fact voice, he recited words which neither Fionn nor any of those who heard them, except the druids, could understand. It was like a verse of poetry: four short lines, which were ended by a little clap of his hands. And at that sound, as if by magic (which is exactly what it was), all those dozens of workers stopped, shuddered. Their eyelids fluttered, their mouths gaped and many of them slumped to the ground, sobbing – but with relief!

The message quickly spread that it was Taoscán who had freed them, and he would have been injured, perhaps, by their frenzied efforts to express their thanks had not Fionn and several of his men gathered round and force-fully, yet kindly, persuaded them to keep a respectful distance from their saviour.

When all was quiet again, the three druids faced Dubhdraoi once more. 'Many things have changed, obviously, since we sat in the same class all those years ago, Dubhdraoi,' began Taoscán. He motioned the prisoner – for that was what he was now, however civilized the conversation might be – towards a seat.

Then Taoscán beckoned Fionn to him, and whispered, 'Well I know that all these standing here would dearly love to hear what we must speak of next. But that cannot be. Do what you think fit.'

That was Taoscán's kind way of saying 'Get them all out of here!' And that is precisely what Fionn did. 'Move! Out! We have a lot o' work in front of us before we can leave here today. Diarmaid, start smashing those ovens. Conán, break them chimneys. Goll, get ready to start levelling that wall outside in the lake. I promised you that job already, didn't I? Lughaidh, lead out these unfortunates . . . these slaves here, an' see they come to no harm.'

Then he smiled at Oscar. 'Don't worry. Your time is coming. I have a special task for you. First, though, the rest o' ye, gather up all these brain-balls an' fling 'em out as far as ye can into the lake. That'll soften 'em once an' for all.'

But Mogh Ruith intervened at this point. 'Do no such thing!' he exclaimed. 'They contain human brains, which must be buried with due respect.'

Fionn blushed. 'Sorry, your honour. With all the excitement, I forgot. Where d'you want 'em brought, so?'

'Why not leave them as they are, and when you give

your orders to Oscar they will have a resting place that is fitting.' And he smiled faintly.

Fionn turned to go, then stopped. But . . . but . . . he had not yet even told Oscar what he wanted him to do – which was, with his enormous strength, to leap, jump up and down and trample the top of the cliff until he collapsed the roofs of the caves in which they now stood, in such a way that they could never again be used.

It gave Fionn no little cause for wonder that this man should know his unspoken thoughts, but when he looked back, Mogh Ruith was gone about other business. 'Just as well to have fellows like that on your side rather than against you,' he mused as he changed his orders: 'Listen! Forget what I said. Leave 'em where they are. Special orders from Mogh Ruith himself.'

And that was done. Yet no one remained idle over the next hour or two; none was made feel neglected. It was sound strategy too, for it gave the quiet necessary for the three druids to retreat to a corner to do what they had to:

Mogh Ruith: 'Why, Dubhdraoi, have you done . . . ' – looking around him – ' . . . this? Profit? Fame? To create fear? To curry favour?'

Fíodh: 'It cannot be. There are easier ways to bring about all of these miserable things. None, surely, who pass through our schools could sink to such pettiness.'

No reply.

Mogh: (almost rising) 'It is your duty to tell us! We demand it. As does your own honour and that of your family.'

No reply.

Taoscán: (softly, seeming to examine a distant cobweb

on the roof over them) 'Do you recall, Dubhdraoi, our teacher of ancient history?'

Dubhdraoi was instantly alert. 'Feidhlim? I do, well. Too well. He was a . . . not a nice man. As well you know. He hated anyone from Leinster – my countrymen.'

Taoscán nodded, but made no answer. The other two, though, were listening intently now. Taoscán continued after a few moments: 'But why this horrible work we see around us here? We all went through various hard times at school.'

Dubhdraoi's face darkened. When he spoke, he spat out the words bitterly. 'You? Or them?' – pointing, mocking and defiant, at his other two accusers. 'Little ye knew about hard times, where ye came from. From the moment I came in that cursed school door, it was hurt, hardship and mockery. At games, in class, even at prayers. I could understand that from stupid idiot boys trying to act like men. But from teachers too? Men of the grey cloak? Men of supposed wisdom? Phah!' He spat.

Fíodh was about to interrupt, but Mogh Ruith, sur-prisingly, motioned him back. 'Go on,' he said to Dubhdraoi.

'I will.' His head drooped, as if he was exhausted. But he recovered and spoke steadily on. 'Which of you cried himself to sleep night after night in that place? Just because my family was not rich, my clothes and shoes not fine, like the other boys, there was gibing, and poking and laughter. And did those so-called teachers ever try to intervene? No, but laughed themselves, called me ugly names in class. To be thought funny . . . though I never failed in any test we were subjected to.'

Taoscán: 'All of them? Surely not . . . '

Dubhdraoi: 'True. Not all. There was one kind man, a teacher of law.'

Taoscán: 'Tuathal?'

Dubhdraoi: 'The very one. A man of culture and civility, if ever such has walked the earth.'

Taoscán nodded, but said only, 'Continue.'

But Fíodh stood now, anger in his voice. 'Must we listen to this kind of nonsense? I, for one, have better things to do.'

And then Taoscán uttered one of those small yet large remarks that had made him famous, trusted, revered in all parts of the land: 'Then you had better go and do them. We will inform you of developments here.'

Fíodh was so taken aback that he sat, blinking, as if stunned. To be spoken to like this . . . by a friend! Before an enemy of humanity such as Dubhdraoi!

Taoscán, though, had motioned that same enemy on again. But in truth, the guilty one was also taken aback. 'Amm . . . I . . . oh yes, Tuathal. An excellent man. If even a few were like him, all would have been bearable.'

Mogh Ruith :   'But why then did you stay?'

Dubhdraoi: 'How could I leave? And shame my family? I, the first of all of us to achieve such an honour?'

There was a long silence between them then. Finally Taoscán spoke. 'What you tell us may have been a cause of what you have done, but how could it be a good reason? Do you not recall, the day you finished, and received your cloak, your promise . . . to use your powers for good only? Could your sufferings, such as they were, not have made you better, stronger, rather than a servant of selfishness and dark will?'

'Easy to say all that here and now,' Dubhdraoi replied.

'And faced by your kind self, I cannot but agree. My only thought, though, at the start, armed with my new powers, was to make, if I could, this world – and the next, too – a misery only for those who had made my life the very same. After that . . . human nature . . . you know it all yourself. How my special, new (though very old) weapon, the brain-ball, was taken up by every chief who wanted a quick leg-up in the world.'

He lapsed into a gloomy silence. What he had to say was said, obviously.

His judges looked at each other, and this time Fíodh was silent. Whether he had changed his opinion was not obvious. Nor did it signify. For this was a matter that would have to be settled not here, but by a higher court, and at Tara, where King Cormac must witness it.

Taoscán rose then, thoughtfully, and moved to where Fionn was watching intently. 'I think we have done all we can for the moment with Dubhdraoi. For the rest, he will accompany us back to Tara. A court of equals must be summoned very soon to decide his fate.'

Fionn nodded. All that was no business of his, and he was glad of it. Too many things could go wrong in dealing with druids, especially for mere fighting men like himself and the Fianna. Better leave magic and such to those trained to deal with it.

'D'ye need any help with him?' he offered, prompt and ready, as always.

'Thanks, but no. You and the others have plenty to do here, I think.' He looked around the chamber. 'I think I heard you saying – or was it Mogh Ruith that told me? – that this place needs some rearranging. Maybe that is what you should see to, while we are on our way, eh?'

'That suits me fine. But could I ask one thing of you?'

'By all means,' smiled Taoscán.

'Will you stay long enough to watch Oscar destroying these caves? He's young, an' it'd make him very pleased. An' also, o' course, you'd be able to check for yourself that the job was done right. You're the one who made this whole thing happen, after all.'

Taoscán agreed, still smiling. 'Yes, I think we can all manage such a delay. It will do my heart good to see it laid to waste.'

Ten more minutes and all was in readiness. Workers, druids, Dubhdraoi and the men of the Fianna stood within clear view of the cliff while Oscar readied himself for this most public show of strength.

But not before Goll had walked out onto the wall surrounding the *dób* mine and surveyed it keenly. He strode back to Fionn. 'I could probably knock it on my own – put my back to it an' push it out, there near the middle of it' – he pointed out the place. 'But if I did that, I'd have water up to my neck before I could do any more. So is it all the same with you, Fionn, if I ask for three men to help me do the job right?'

Fionn could see that it went very much against the grain for Goll to have to make this request, and share his glory. But he had to admire the man's common sense. ''Tis a good man who knows when he needs help, Goll. Take whoever you want.'

Naturally, he chose his brother Conán, and also Mac Lughach and Diarmaid.

In a few minutes, the four warriors were in position,

backs to the wall. Then Goll gave his command: 'Right, men! Push! Heeeave!'

And push they did, almost bursting their buttons, while those watching shouted and groaned encouragement, all in the best of good humour: 'Weaklings! Come on! Wouldn't a crowd o' children lift that, never mind pushing it down!'

For several moments, nothing moved, then inch by inch it began to bulge and buckle outward, then topple into the lake beyond. Still they strained, though the water was now gushing around and over them.

'Keep at it !' Goll roared, but he had no need to. None of them wanted to be first from his post, and it was only when they had either to swim or drown that they struck out for shore at last, to the clapping and cheers of all the watchers.

The water had well and truly submerged the *dób* diggings, poured into and flooded the caves when Fionn signalled to Oscar, who was waiting, relaxed, on the clifftop. 'Begin!' Fionn shouted.

And Oscar did: he leaped ten feet into the air and landed straight and rigid as a battering ram. Again and again, up and down, here, there and yon on that clifftop over the cave-roof. After almost two dozen such hammer blows, he paused. 'Aha! One or two more'll do it, I'd say. I can feel it cracking.'

'Make sure you don't fall in yourself when it collapses,' warned Fionn. ''Tis no part of our job to have to dig you out.'

No sooner had he said it than the warning became reality. A hole – widening by the second – opened, and, with a muffled rumble and clatter, the ground began to unravel and disappear. Luckily for Oscar, he had several feet of a margin, and he used it by leaping to safety and then staggering a few steps further back again.

A shout of triumph from the shore and round about greeted the collapse, and Fionn was just about to order the men forward to complete the destruction when the thunder of hooves and a blare of horns signified that they were no longer alone.

Through the trees now streamed horsemen from several directions until all the space at every side of the collapse was occupied. Their leader was tall, bristling with hair and weapons: a hard-looking nail. Not a man to be trifled with.

The newcomer swung from the saddle, angrily. 'Who are ye? Who gave ye permission to set foot on my land? To dare desecrate an inch of it?'

Fionn stepped forward. 'Chief O'Neill of Clanna Buí, is it yourself? Right glad we are to see your noble person here.'

'Fionn Mac Cumhail! An' the rest o' your . . . gang. What business have you in – ?'

He did not finish, for as he looked furiously about him, he caught sight of the four druids standing to one side together, silent. He recognised them at once and stopped. His tone changed in an instant.

'Oh . . . your . . . your honours. I never saw ye there. Ye're more than welcome to my poor domain.' As they did not speak at once, he added foolishly, 'An' if there's something I or my people can do . . . ' His voice trailed off nervously. He could see clearly now from the downcast appearance of Dubhdraoi that all was not as it should be.

Taoscán stepped forward, unsmiling. 'Chief O'Neill, I

will not waste words. Why did you not reply to King Cormac's letter, and why have you allowed this place, this work, to thrive within your lands? When word of these ignoble deeds spreads, how can it reflect but ill upon the name O'Neill? This man here' – pointing to Dubhdraoi – 'is in your employ, is he not? And that one there' – picking out Maelgarbh – 'one of your sub-chiefs?'

O'Neill nodded. 'Yes, but whatever is being done here I know nothing about. I swear it, on my mother's grave. Dubhdraoi told me he was making a new kind of eel jelly. An' why wouldn't I believe him? All last winter we had it at every feast, an' you'd eat your fingers after it. But Maelgarbh, he told me nothing. An' as for a letter from King Cormac, I never got any such letter.'

'Hmmm. It appears you are not quite as much in control of your dominions as you thought,' mused Taoscán, looking steadily at the trees over O'Neill's shoulder. 'All may be as you say. But have no fear, we will find the truth. And for that, Dubhdraoi must accompany us to Tara. Maelgarbh we leave to you to question.'

'Yes, yes, o' course,' O'Neill nodded, full of anxiety to help now. 'Whatever you say. An' if there's anything else . . .'

'There is,' Taoscán cut in. 'You see this place here? Make certain that this hole is fully filled. In such a way that it will not be used again. Fionn will leave ten men to help in any way you wish.'

The interview was over, and no matter what resentment or anger may have been in O'Neill's mind, he strove to push it from him. He knew all too well the uncanny knack druids had of reading minds, revealing the most hidden, secret thoughts, like ants beneath a stone. He knew too that the ten men were to make certain that brain-balls would never again be made here. But what was to be done? Nothing. And better to accept it with a smile, no matter how painted-on.

'They'll be welcome,' the chief said. 'An' if they'd like to stay for a bit o' hunting, dancing or whatever, they're welcome to that too.'

'I'd expect no less from an O'Neill,' nodded Taoscán, returning quietly to where the others still stood, silent.

There was no more to be done at that place by the druids; they made a discreet departure a short time later, but not before Taoscán had warned Fionn about the ten men needed: 'Pick only those who will not be influenced by anything except your orders. This place must never again be what it has been.'

Those ten were quickly chosen, Diarmaid among them to make sure that all was done properly, and Cairbre too. It would be useful experience for him to see how such a task was completed.

Then Fionn straightened himself. 'All right,' he said. 'We'll start for Tara.'

He bowed to O'Neill, then turned sharply and marched off, followed by the twenty-seven others in line – the envy of the men of Uladh for their soldierly stance, civilised but utterly dangerous.

It was a journey far different from those of the previous two days – steady but not forced, full of talk and laughter – and no little wonder at the latest they had witnessed of the druids' powers:

'Lord, but isn't it a foolish man too, that'd put himself

up against 'em,' Diarmaid said of his companions.

'I don't know about that,' said Fionn, teasing. 'If there was a bit o' real intelligence, now, behind some o' that wrongdoing, an' not just the same oul' stupid greed, power an' the rest of it, it'd be a lot harder to get the better of it.'

'Why don't you try a bit o' crime yourself, Fionn?' laughed Oisín. 'We'd all follow you, if it came to it. With the oxter-bag an' your thumb o' knowledge, you should be a good enough match for 'em, eh?'

But that conversation had gone far enough. Fionn waved his hand. 'Ah, stop talking gibberish, will ye?' and despite all efforts, joking and serious, he refused to continue with that subject any further. He knew why, too: because he had often, arriving home to the Hill of Allen, exhausted, complaining to Maighnis of the impossible demands being made of him by Cormac, been advised quietly by that so-sane woman, 'Take the whole thing into your own hands, why don't you! You're doing most o' the work anyway, aren't you?'

She was right, he knew. He should. But . . . his best, most respected friend, Taoscán – how would he react? Fionn did not – and never would – want to put him in a position of having to make such a choice.

And that, basically, was why he laughed now. 'Keep going, men, an' talk about home or something nice like that,' he said then. 'Ye don't want me to give the order for silence, do ye?'

He may have laughed, but they knew he was serious, so conversation faded. But not for long, because as they passed the various places where he had promised them stories on their way north, these promises he was now reminded of, every one. And being a man of his word, he did not refuse.

As they paused a moment at their late campsite on its rocky hill, Fionn announced, 'Ye might remember that I mentioned Tnúthán in this place.'

'Indeed we do,' they shouted together.

'Well, if 'tis all the same to ye, I'll keep it until tonight in Tara, where we'll have comfort, *poitín* an' good food to make the hearing of it even better.'

'No, no! We want it now,' they roared, but when he pointed out a huge bank of dark cloud creeping towards them from the west, they began to think again.

'An' I'll throw in the one about the burning of Lios Liath for good measure,' he added, to soothe them. 'But we'd better be going on now, an' maybe we'll get to shelter with the Fir Rois, before that cloud drenches us.'

They did that. The first drops in a downpour that lasted nearly two hours accompanied them through the gateway of the first of those friendly chiefs, and by the time they were ready for the road again, Fionn had been forced to tell a little of 'The Burning of Lios Liath' – a little only, though, because in its entirety it was a story that demanded half a night for its proper telling.

But when the rain stopped, he stopped also, at a most exciting part of the action, and no promises of gold or cattle could make him continue. Well he understood the power of suspense! 'No,' he said. 'We're needed back at Tara. But,' he promised, 'ye're welcome at my house on the Hill of Allen this night week, an' I'll guarantee to finish it, every word. Sure I'm only starting it yet.'

They were delighted. 'We'll be there, never fear,' and

once more they took to the road.

At the Boyne crossing, after they had crept silently past Sídh i mBroga – far more sinister now in the dark – it was the same: 'I'll tell all ye want to know tonight at Tara.'

But there was one story they did not ask for – 'The Death of Múchán' – though he knew they longed to hear it. It was only when they were within sight of the lights of Tara that he cautioned them: 'Let no one ask any question about Múchán until His Highness has asked first. That privilege is his. An' Diarmaid must be told also, when he comes back. Maybe the surprise of Mogh Ruith's an' Fíodh Mac Neimhe's visit will keep such talk away until I can consider how best to tell the news to each in turn.'

'Why? How d'you mean?'

'Cormac is the one, remember, who must set a price on his life, an' sentence Dubhdraoi accordingly – as well as for his other evil deeds – after he gets advice from the druids.'

It was with such to think on that they arrived home at last, another mission accomplished. And they were welcomed in royal fashion.

Cormac was at the lit-up northern gate, arms wide, smiling his smile of triumph in the blaze of a hundred torches. Taoscán was on his left, Mogh Ruith and Fíodh standing severely behind, all others in the shadows at a discreet distance. But where was Dubhdraoi?

'Ye have done great service to Tara again,' intoned Cormac, 'and will be honoured accordingly.' Then, as he threw his arms impressively around Fionn, he whispered, far less formally, 'Where's Cairbre? Is he all right? Did he make a *gamal* of himself? Tell me!'

And Fionn, under cover of a subject's extra-loving

embrace, murmured back, 'Far, far from it, Your Highness. He did all expected of a prince, an' more. Without him, twenty men who still breathe might not be alive, including myself.'

Cormac was visibly shaken. 'You're not telling me lies, Fionn, are you?'

'Not one, Your Highness. He's a boy I'd take with me again. What better can I say?'

'Come in, quick, an' tell me all about it.'

Fionn noticed . . . was it a tear in Cormac's eye? But he himself said no more, showed no emotion, only bowed, stepped back formally. He knew Cormac's changeable moods far too well to become entirely involved here. One hour wrath, the next hour love: he had seen it all before. So he smiled, though his praise of Cairbre was quite sincere.

'I'll be right after you, Your Highness, as soon as I give these men their orders.'

Cormac strode off, smiling, rubbing his hands briskly. Those who had remained at Tara noticed his bright mood.

'What has him so pleased, Fionn?'

'Ye'll find out, don't worry. Just enjoy it while it lasts.'

He hurried to Taoscán then, bowed quickly to the other two. 'I'm sorry to even seem to neglect ye, but ye know how 'tis.'

Taoscán laughed, nodded. 'Have no worry about that. Only come down to my place as soon as you may.'

'I'll be there, never fear.'

They left him then, and he went about what any commander must – orders, arrangements, the fobbing off of pointless questions: 'Ye'll hear all about it at the feast tonight. How many times have I to tell ye, let no one put himself before the king – it could be dangerous.'

When all these formalities were completed and commands given for the next few busy hours' happenings, Fionn made his way towards the royal quarters. This kind of visit made him more nervous than any battle-charge, close combat or head-counting.

But he was pleasantly surprised by Cormac's welcome. At the door he was grasped by the hand, ushered inside in a mannerly way that was . . . genuine, he felt! Mead was poured for him by the royal right hand, he was seated in the seat of honour, next to the royal bed, and the questions began.

'Are you sure, Fionn, that Cairbre did as you told me out there? You weren't *plámás*ing me, I hope.'

'I was not, Your Highness. You'll find that out when you talk to the other men – an' they all saw as much as I did.'

'Of course, of course. For every man his own honour, I always say. Not a one o' 'em but will have his time of praise – if Cairbre was as good as you tell me.'

Fionn grimaced. Why could he not accept that his son had at least some of the qualities that might one day make him a worthy king? Jealousy? Fear?

'He was. I'll put my word of honour on that, if you wish.'

'No, no need for that. I believe you, I do.' He began to pace the chamber then, lips moving in some silent conversation with himself, as if he were quite alone.

At last Fionn could take no more. He rose. 'I must go down to meet Taoscán, Your Highness. Himself, Mogh

Ruith an' Fíodh Mac Neimhe are men that may not be kept waiting. There is much to be talked of before all is revealed in the great hall this night.'

Mention of that seemed to jolt Cormac out of his daydream, trance . . . whatever it was. He stood, motionless. 'Yes . . . yes. We had better go down.'

'We?' thought Fionn. But now was hardly the time to argue.

They made their way uninterrupted, though keenly watched, to Taoscán's cave, where the door was open, obviously for them. Inside sat Taoscán in his usual seat, comfortable, at home. At either side sat Mogh Ruith and Fíodh. No one moved. Nor did Cormac, at the door. Here was where the pomp and power of kingship ran out. That much even he knew well. Within these walls only the final, basic things mattered: truth, honour, friendship. There would be no deceit here, no flattery, no self-serving.

'Within the hour, King Cormac – question not the how, you know the why – the druids of the five provinces will gather here to pass sentence on Dubhdraoi. Crimes like his – '

'Wait! Hold on!' Cormac had come to life. 'Where is he? The man has to be present to defend himself, surely.'

'Oh, he is present, never fear.' It was Mogh Ruith who said it, in a voice as cold as ice. And suitable that was too, for when he rose, slowly, almost sinisterly, and motioned to his left, they saw in that corner a block of . . . what looked like ice, a man frozen within it – yet not quite ice. There was something to it: a brownness, a shadow. Yet even in the lamplight they could see clear enough the shocked face, the clenched fingers, the half-attempted run.

'Where did he think he'd be escaping to?' thought Fionn. 'Once druids like these come after you, 'tis as well to spare yourself trouble an' give up. An' the sooner the better.'

'What we need most of all during his trial is quietness,' said Taoscán, sombrely now.

'An' privacy, I s'pose,' added Fionn.

'No. This very matter we have discussed, and we think it best that justice be seen to be done openly, for fear of talk of favouritism and such.'

The other two nodded.

'The great hall would be the best place. There everyone may sit according to rank.'

That seemed fair, and Fionn called one of the guards, gave him immediate orders for Murchadh Maor to have the hall prepared: lights, seating, tables and all else that was needed. 'Should we send out messengers to all the chiefs around?' Fionn asked then.

'No!' snapped Mogh Ruith. 'This is not a show or spectacle. Those who are here when we begin will be lookers-on enough.'

Fionn stepped back, said no more. But he could not help thinking what a difference in manner there was between Taoscán and this man, whom he found himself taking a sharp dislike to.

As Taoscán had said, the druids of the five provinces arrived at Tara in no more than an hour, each one looking grim, with little time for pleasantries, only a curtsy and a few words for Cormac.

Before the doors could be closed, though, Fionn asked Taoscán, 'Would it please ye to wait a little while, for

Diarmaid an' the others we left behind to make sure your job at Loch Neacach was finished properly by O'Neill?'

'Provided they aren't too long, I think I can persuade my friends to do that.'

Fionn smiled his thanks, then called Caoilte urgently. 'Go north, will you, as fast as your legs'll move, meet 'em on the way – they can't be too far off now – an' tell 'em hurry or they'll miss the trial.'

Caoilte needed no more telling. In a few moments, he was streaking off out of sight in a shower of spatters.

His efforts were hardly needed, though. Just south of the Boyne crossing he met them marching at a steady tramp towards him, gasped out his instructions and was briefly thanked. Diarmaid spoke then: 'It won't be us that'll delay the course o' justice this night, men. Quicken up an' we'll be there in an hour, or even less.'

Meanwhile at Tara, the judges had settled themselves along the length of the top table in the hall while two special chairs – one for Cormac, the other for Cairbre – had been prepared in front, between it and the other watchers. Taoscán had insisted on the second. Proper that the prince should see justice dispensed at first-hand – if he arrived in time, that is.

In the period of waiting there was much shuffling, dark whispering and earnest gesturing behind the top table, but down in the hall the one question in every mouth was: 'Where is he, this . . . this brain-ball man? Has he two heads, or four legs, or why are they hiding him from us?'

Taoscán overheard these growlings too, for he motioned Fionn to him. 'I know they're all excited down there, Fionn. But we must have quietness here to discuss this case. So rather than put everyone out, why don't you go down to my rooms, bring up Dubhdraoi as you find him – just as you saw him – and place him there' – pointing to the empty floor-space – 'where everyone may look their fill. You will know what to tell them.' And his old eyes twinkled.

Fionn almost laughed. In the midst of such a serious affair, this venerable man, as always, knew better than anyone how people think, react, behave. The leader of the Fianna moved at once, nudging Oscar forward before him, across the courtyard, out and down the hill. At the cave, he knew what he was looking for, where to look. But when Oscar saw the strange ice-pillar, and its even stranger contents, he hesitated, naturally.

Luckily, Fionn was to hand. 'No questions now,' he said shortly. 'Move this up with me, that's all.'

And it was done, though uncomfortably, for even in the dark, that frozen look, that piercing stare from the icy block seemed to follow Oisín, though he tried and tried again to avoid it. He was relieved – shaking a little, though he would not have admitted it – when they set it down at last in the space between judges and onlookers.

Of course it was the focus of all attention from the moment it was placed there – largely from the benches below, but with not a few glances from the judges also, as Fionn observed. But mainly it did what Taoscán knew it would – gave a respite until Diarmaid and the others could arrive.

And arrive they did, all of an hour later, breathless. It took minutes only for the doorkeepers of the hall to advise them of what was in progress within.

'I think we should stay out here, entirely, Diarmaid,' hinted Conán.

'That's what I'd feel too, but they're waiting for us, an' not to go in wouldn't be mannerly. Just to show we're still alive, if nothing else.' And so they sought entry.

There was no applause as they made their way silently – almost nervously – up the hall, but they could see clearly enough that every eye was following them, not least Cormac's. Which might have been expected, for naturally he was waiting, all excited, for his son's appearance. And Cairbre was hardly inside the door when his father did a most unkingly thing: leaped up, scurried around the nearest bench and flung his arms round the prince's neck – much to the young man's embarrassment.

But Fionn's words of praise were still ringing in the king's ears. He was proud of his boy, he was going to show it, and that was that! 'You're welcome home,' he beamed, 'an' the rest o' ye too. Ye have done well, an' we thank ye.'

They were soon seated, relieved to be here at last – and in time, too, for the trial.

It was not long in starting. A slight hint of a nod from Taoscán, and Fionn brought the hall to order. 'Silence, everyone!' he intoned. 'From now on, let no one talk unless he's spoken to.'

In the hush that followed, Taoscán rose slowly and began the accusation without any introduction. 'Him you see here before you has been brought this night to answer grave charges. Acts have been committed here at Tara – ye all knew Siascán, did ye not? – that cannot be let pass unanswered. But not at Tara only. Those who have returned from Loch Neacach this very hour could – and will, no doubt – tell of deeds most horrible, knowledge misused, pity and mercy scorned.'

'But how'll he answer if he's stuck inside in that block of ice, or whatever 'tis?' asked Dlúthach.

Fionn glared at the questioner, but Taoscán was not annoyed. 'He will be allowed to speak for himself, have no fear of that. But we have questioned him already. We know enough about his handiwork to pass sentence . . . right . . . now.'

The deliberate way he said it impressed the listeners, for they knew him to be a man not given to great showiness of speech.

'Yet,' he continued, 'we will not do so until you too have heard him, and especially' – turning to Cormac – 'Your Highness.' He sat then, leaving the audience silent, straining forward to see better what was to come. Even Fionn wondered what the next step might be.

He need not have worried, for the druids had another surprise in store. For a moment they looked at each other wordlessly, then, as one, turned their gaze on Dubhdraoi. Silent, unmoving, they stared at the block which held him trapped. In the hush of that moment, a cat's padding through the hall would have been counted loud.

And then an extraordinary thing happened. Steam – or was it smoke? who could tell! – began to curl from the ice. But only from that part of it surrounding Dubhdraoi's head. And still it rose, until, exposed for all to see, were the dark features of the villain himself.

Every onlooker waited breathless for the storm of words which they felt must come – of fright, hatred or pleading. In short, all the reactions they would have expected of themselves. But they were disappointed. Whatever else he might be, Dubhdraoi was still a druid, and the discipline of his training remained with him even now. Not a move did he make when Mogh Ruith asked formally, 'Have you anything to say in your defence?' A pause, then Mogh Ruith added, 'Speak now or never.'

Still nothing. The audience was amazed.

'Isn't he a bold one?' marvelled Goll.

'Or maybe he has some surprise of his own prepared,' whispered Conán.

'Inside in that ice? Sure what can he do with only his head sticking out?'

'Yerra, will you have sense, man! Isn't it in his head all the spells are.'

Before there could be any more speculation – even before Fionn could order the whisperers to be silent – Taoscán looked Dubhdraoi in the eye: 'Then the time has come for us to do what is our duty.'

Dubhdraoi did not flinch as he said it, only watched them unblinking as they trooped out to their private consulting chamber.

'This will not take long,' Fíodh nodded to Cormac, leaving him alone at the top of the hall except for Fionn.

But he was wrong. And as minutes passed into an hour, and that into two, then three, every kind of guesswork and speculation began to do the rounds of the hall.

'Boy oh boy, but they must be trying to count the number o' pieces they'll chop him up into.'

'Not at all, man! They're arguing about how deep they'll bury him alive.'

'Or drown him, maybe?'

'I doubt that. It'd be too easy. Maybe they'll put him

down into the roots of an oak tree, like was done to Galar in Coill Cam.'[4]

The remembrance of that horrible episode quieted them for a little while, but when, in a further half an hour, there was still no sign, even Fionn began to get restless.

'Could there be anything wrong, d'you think?' he asked Cormac.

The king shrugged. 'I hope not. I don't want to be left with the responsibility of executing that lad there' – staring at Dubhdraoi, who immediately answered with an even darker glare of his own.

'I think he heard you,' murmured Fionn.

'Let him hear,' snapped Cormac. 'This is my house, is it not?'

'Yes, but he isn't exactly what you'd call a guest, is he?' Fionn smiled. 'I don't think the rules of hospitality apply in this case.'

They lapsed into silence then, fingering the cutlery, each thinking his own thoughts, and only when the consulting-room door was wrenched open fifteen minutes later did a flurry of life return.

As each druid emerged, he was scrutinised closely, in the hope of guessing where his vote had gone. And yes, there were some angry, flushed faces, while others gave nothing away. Only Taoscán was smiling.

The druids took their places, and while they settled themselves, Cormac whispered to Taoscán out of the corner of his mouth: 'Should I say something, or leave it to yourself?'

'You're the master of the house. It is your entitlement to speak first.'

Cormac nodded, then rose. All attention focused on him immediately.

'*A dhaoine uaisle,*' he began, nodding to left and right, 'we have waited eagerly for this moment – a moment of decision for Dubhdraoi in particular. Your judgement we do not doubt; your wisdom we cannot question. Deliver your decision.'

As he sat, Taoscán rose. But so did Mogh Ruith. The onlookers were surprised, yet interested too. This was unusual, to say the least.

Taoscán began. 'We cannot, therefore we will not, pretend that our decision as regards Dubhdraoi and his misdeeds has been as unanimous as I would have wished, but – '

He was interrupted by Mogh Ruith – ignorantly, Fionn thought, but he kept that thought to himself. 'You express it very mildly, comrade Mac Liath. If your persuasive tongue had not inclined others of lesser conviction in your direction, this wretch before us would not trouble the land of Ireland again for seven times seven generations.' He sat down abruptly, temper showing in all his features.

'True,' sighed Taoscán mildly. 'But what then? As I have said and said already, why should we, here and now, burden the people of Ireland centuries hence with an evil that is ours, which can be ended here?'

'I only hope you're right,' growled Mogh Ruith ominously. 'Be it on your own head if you are not.'

'Yes indeed. Indeed,' mused Taoscán, fingertips to his lips, all his attention trained now on the one in the ice.

He paced out into the floor-space then and addressed Dubhdraoi. His voice was soft, but in it was steel far more dangerous than sharpest sword or spear most keen. 'You realise, I hope, that your friends here are few – yet not so few as to deprive you of one last chance to redeem yourself.'

Dubhdraoi said nothing, only stared. Yet Taoscán noted that he was listening carefully, all the same.

'I will not waste words. We have decided' – he faced the audience as he said it, but gazed at the roof-beams – 'not to resort to any of the punishments that might be expected here this night. In fact, Dubhdraoi, your sentence is far more severe – though how much more depends entirely on yourself.'

The audience was all ears now. What could this mean?

'Trust druids to put a twist in everything,' hissed Goll.

'Shhh! Or they'll put a twist in you too.'

'You are sentenced,' Taoscán continued, 'under pain of immediate, undying shame, to go forth, when daylight comes, from this hall and for the remainder of your days to help the poor, the homeless, the sick and the mad. Within three days, you start at Gleann na nGealt in Corca Dhuibhne. How you do it and with whom from then on is your affair – except that you may not bewitch, enchant or force anyone to help you against their will.'

A strange expression – confusion perhaps, as well as surprise – passed over Dubhdraoi's face. He would, no doubt, have scratched his head if his hand had been free to do so.

But the look of bemusement on his face was nothing compared to the reaction from below. Eyes blinked, brows furrowed, fingers clenched tables as the listeners tried to come to terms with what they had heard.

Caoilte, one of Múchán's closest friends, leaped to his feet then. Whatever about Fionn's commanded silence, he was angry and was going to have his say. 'Am I hearing right? Sure this is no punishment at all, only a holiday about Ireland for him.'

A mighty nodding of heads and much muttering all about showed that most of the audience agreed with the prince.

But Taoscán, never one to give way to a crowd, no matter how large or vocal, merely added, 'It will not be so simple for him as might appear. He will have cold, loneliness and darkness as his companions for much of the time that lies before him.'

'An' what's to stop him escaping to the Eastern World or somewhere else?'

'Or to brew more badness in that evil mind of his?'

'Us,' answered Taoscán simply. 'Any such attempt, and his memory will be taken from him, and all his power and learning. He will be condemned to wander the roads a fool and be laughed at, tormented like those poor mad ones he is now to help. And mockery, whether you know it or not, is the bitterest medicine for anyone of our brotherhood to bear.'

Silent, they considered his words, and true enough, they had to admit that none of them had ever seen a druid laughed at.

But Caoilte was not satisfied. 'What about an honour-price for Múchán? Surely King Cormac is owed that much for the loss of such a brave man?'

'I will not speak for His Highness,' said Taoscán. 'That choice is his, and his only.'

The druid sat, and all attention shifted to the king. And surprisingly, for once, Cormac gave a judgement both quick and wise – in other words, he repeated what Taoscán had just said, and merely added, 'My honour will be satisfied if he does all that he is commanded.'

'Too easy he is to satisfy,' mumbled Caoilte, but his master had spoken and that was that.

Mogh Ruith now addressed Dubhdraoi shortly. 'To-morrow morning you will be released, then banished to your punishment – '

'"Task" I would prefer to call it,' Taoscán corrected him. 'For there is great need in Ireland of helping the mad especially, since there are so many of them.'

'Oh! A dirty dig there,' thought Fionn, but he let well be, since Cormac seemed to have missed it.

Food and drink were ordered, now that this awkward business had been disposed of. And it was willingly brought, for the servants, though exhausted now, were burning with curiosity to find out what had been the outcome of this long affair.

But if Fionn thought that feasting or tiredness might cause his men to forget the stories he had promised them, he had another think coming. With their usual love of any promise of possible gore, mystery and a good tale, he was pursued now, in geographical order, south to north, for each of those expected tellings.

And he did not disappoint. From the account of his fearsome encounter at Sídh i mBroga (which lasted all of three hours, and after which there was at least half an hour's respectful silence and copious draughts of *poitín* to help the story down) to the telling of Tnúthán's grisly fate, to the origin of the rocky headland at Aill Bhuí, he kept them bug-eyed and open-mouthed by turns, especially King Cormac, until it was broad daylight. Even the druids were impressed, for not one of those serious men left; rather, they seemed to relax into this unaccustomed kind of enjoyment now that their real work was finished.

But the most fascinated spectator of all, if anyone had observed (which no one did), was Dubhdraoi, standing there ignored in his block of ice. He hid it well, though – all except his eyes, which remained fixed on Fionn all the while he was speaking.

And in all that time, there was only one interruption. A good hour into the Tnúthán story, when that villain's defeat was by no means yet sure, there was a sudden 'Awkh-squawkkh!' half-way down the hall, and Conán leaped to his feet.

'What in the . . . !' snarled Fionn, angry to be interrupted. But there, clinging for dear life to the edge of the table, was a shivering, bug-eyed white bird, looking much the worse for wear.

Men rose, heads craned. Even the druids were curious. 'What's that, Conán?' demanded Taoscán.

'Oh . . . am . . . I forgot about him,' the bald one stammered. 'I had him in my pocket since the time we were going north.'

While Fionn stood there, all attention gone from him for the moment, Taoscán went and picked up the bird gently. 'This creature has been frightened nearly to death,' he said.

There were several sniggers. 'You're right there, Taoscán. If only you knew!'

But by now Fionn had had enough. 'D'ye want to hear the story or talk about an oul' bird? Make up yeer minds.'

'Sorry, Fionn, but a creature like this must have its moment too. Continue,' and the druid took his place again, soothing the bird, softly, gently.

And Fionn did continue, quickly silencing the crowd once more.

By the time he had finished his account of the making of Aill Bhuí, though, his voice was beginning to fray, so he was glad when Diarmaid noticed this and called Murchadh to bring in the breakfast.

That was seen to, amid huge applause for Fionn. Even Dubhdraoi smiled, though as before it passed unnoticed by all – except, on this occasion, by Taoscán. 'There's hope for that man yet,' he nodded silently. 'I only hope he will use his opportunity well.'

Just before noon, when Dubhdraoi was released from his block of ice, everyone in Tara was present to see the event. Silent they stood, in the yard, on the battlements, while he was lifted out of the hall to face his judges again. No word was spoken between them. As they had done before, so now again – a concentrated stare . . . and the block began to melt, inch by inch.

Only when the last of the smoke . . . or steam . . . had vanished did Mogh Ruith speak. Dourly, too. 'Go. And you will be watched. Always remember that.'

Dubhdraoi only looked at him, then stepped forward to Taoscán, sank to one knee and grasped his hand. 'Thank you.' It was all he said – the last words any of those standing there would ever hear him speak at Tara.

He left then, with neither companion nor belongings, and the whole crowd continued to stare at him almost until he was out of sight. No one passed any comment – they knew better! – until Cormac it was who finally announced lamely, 'Well, that's that, I s'pose', and they all moved back into the hall, carefully avoiding the place where the block of ice had stood.

Of more immediate concern, though, was the burial ceremony for Múchán. And a royal send-off he received too, with no fewer than eight druids to chant his spirit safe into the world beyond and the High King himself to proclaim his noble deeds and unfailing loyalty.

He was cremated then and his ashes laid with all possible respect near (but not too near!) Sídh i mBroga – a high honour indeed.

It was while returning side by side with Taoscán from this final salute to their fallen friend that Fionn, of a sudden, remembered something. 'By the Lord Lugh!' he exclaimed, clapping his fist to his forehead. 'I nearly forgot!'

Taoscán stopped, looking concerned. 'Are you all right, Fionn? Look, I can understand it if you're upset about Múchán. We all are, but – '

'No, no, 'tisn't that at all' – he rummaged in an inside pocket a few moments – 'but this . . . or these, I should say. I clean forgot to give 'em to you before now.' And he held out the two dark necklaces with their snake-knot medallions.

Taoscán gazed at them, then took them quietly. 'I'm glad you brought these back, Fionn. For, having them, I will make certain that the evil of the brain-ball is truly at an end. Thank you.'

He explained no more, but Fionn knew that the medallions were in the safest of hands now.

Back again in the courtyard at Tara, men crowded around Fionn. 'You're not forgetting about next week, now, are you?' cried Lorcan, obviously the spokesman for all the others.

'How d'you mean?' replied Fionn innocently, though he knew full well what was meant.

'The story, o' course! The rest o' 'The Burning of Lios Liath'! There isn't a single person here in Tara that doesn't want to hear it. All of it – from the start!'

'Hold on a minute, now. I can't invite everyone. How could we leave King Cormac here alone? An' what'd Maighnis say? The Fir Rois are all coming, so how could I make room for everyone?'

Fionn was becoming alarmed now, and worse was to follow, for just then Cormac strolled forth from the back of the crowd, grinning. Obviously he had been listening. 'Another story, Fionn, an' no invitation for me, Mogh Ruith, Fíodh an' the others? I'm surprised at you. If that's the case, I'll have to invite myself.' He was smiling as he said it – which meant he had some mischief in mind.

'Oh . . . Your Highness is more than welcome. An' the others too. I'm sure Maighnis'll be overjoyed to see ye.'

He was quite sure that she would be no such thing, but Cormac was speaking again, in oily tones. 'It does my heart good to hear that. I look forward to seeing her, an' hearing you.'

And off he went, to his chamber, well satisfied.

When Fionn broke this news to Maighnis three hours later, she was aghast, but recovered quickly. 'Trust you to make a pig's ear o' the thing,' she scolded him, but when she saw his hangdog expression, she brightened. 'Well, never mind. At least I have a week to get the place ready.'

She did, too. Worked the servants to the bone for those few days, supervised everything personally, so that when the crowd began to stream towards Allen on the appointed evening, everything was in readiness, for high and low alike.

Fionn marvelled at her efficiency – 'If she was in charge at Tara instead of Murchadh, we'd never have a problem' – but he said it to himself. No point in praising her publicly. That might be seen as boasting – or, worse again, encouragement.

But if Fionn said nothing in her favour, everyone else did. She was showered not only with compliments, but gifts also, each of which she received with a quiet dignity – which only increased her stature in the guests' eyes.

'That's a woman an' a half you have there, Fionn.'

'Why don't you bring her to Tara now an' again? Is it hiding her you are?'

And much more in a similar vein.

Between her management and Fionn's stories, it was an entertainment that was remembered long in the minds and annals of that part of Ireland – not least because, while it lasted, Tara was well-nigh deserted. If any enemies had chosen to attack just then . . . But that is mere idle speculation. None did, for to take advantage of a story-telling to settle private or public quarrel or enmity was regarded as the equivalent of spitting at a druid, or murdering an honest man in his sleep – a cause of personal infamy and family dishonour for seven generations.

And when it was over at last and the guests began their stagger home, they took with them their own stories of the night's proceedings – which was a little unfortunate, for now all those who had not been invited began to raise their voices.

'Is it so we're not good enough, or what?' complained the O'Connors.

'How are the Fir Rois more worthy than we are!' exclaimed McCarthy Mór.

'Is Fionn Mac Cumhail trying to make little of us? 'Cos if he is . . . ' said Ó Flátharta Gorm darkly.

These angry growlings soon made their way (as they were intended to) to Fionn's ears, and to avoid any ill will or feelings of neglect on anyone's part, he had it proclaimed at Tara – with Cormac's sanction, of course – that the same night every other year would become a story-night at the Hill of Allen, where the best tellers from the five provinces might come to mesmerise their audience, if they could.

It was a huge success, too, but in true Irish fashion it began to stretch. Soon it expanded to three nights, then to a week, the intervening days being filled with hunting (when the weather permitted), sightseeing, chess and discussion of strategy, battle alliances and marriages for the coming year. So popular did it become that it would have lengthened even further had not Fionn begged Cormac to stop it at that, 'Before they eat everything I have!'

A week it remained thereafter, looked forward to by one and all, fostering the craft of storytelling to un-dreamed-of heights in the land of Ireland, a distinction it held for almost fifteen centuries thereafter.

And Dubhdraoi? In his case, Mogh Ruith's misgivings were proved to be completely misplaced, for within a year amazing stories began to reach Tara about his doings at Gleann na nGealt: the hostel he had established there for the comforting of the insane ones of the land, the throngs of people (afflicted and sane alike) hurrying thither to see this wonder. Even more startling were the accounts of all those whose scattered wits were restored there. Soon, disciples, impressed by the man's goodness and power, began to build themselves beehive huts round about the hostel, until there was a sizeable settlement in that place.

But instead of basking in all this attention, as he might have done, Dubhdraoi, as soon as he had trained enough of his followers in the treatment of disturbed minds, moved on, to one part of Ireland after another – never to the territory of O'Neill or the vicinity of Tara, though.

'He must be up to something,' was Mogh Ruith's suspicious opinion.

But Taoscán did not agree. 'No. Every man, even the worst, has good in him somewhere, if only it can be brought up into the light.'

He was right, for during the remaining years of his long life, Dubhdraoi's instructions to his many followers never varied: 'Kindness, understanding and patience. Practise them always. Make them your rules, no matter what, and all will be well. Those three were shown to me by a wise man. They saved me from myself, from the madness of the Dark, when school should have done it but did not. The very opposite, indeed.'

But at least his ill experience in the druids' training school had one positive and powerful effect: there was a root-and-branch reorganisation there, a hunting-out of bullying of all kinds. Taoscán himself it was who drew up the new rules, and such was the respect in which he was held that they were accepted by one and all. More importantly, they worked, for never again in the school's illustrious history was there another case like Dubhdraoi's, and eventually students flocked to Ireland from all parts of the known world to be educated by the men of the grey cloak.

And when St Patrick arrived, should we be surprised that the Irish were so receptive to the message he was preaching? Hardly, for in a way the three Divine Virtues, or something very close to them, were already well known, thanks to Dubhdraoi. Nor was the later notion of religious orders at all strange, for the disciples of the same Dubhdraoi, dedicated to the unfortunate, the miserable, the needy, were by then spread over all parts of the land.

GLOSSARY OF IRISH WORDS

Abha Mhór	the Ulster Blackwater
a dhaoine uaisle	formal, rather impersonal greeting – literally 'noble people'
Aill Bhuí	the Yellow Cliff
Airghialla Oriel	an area corresponding roughly to parts of modern Meath, east Monaghan and Louth
Árd Mór	literally 'the Great Height'
A thiarna!	*('Lord!')* expression of surprise or amazement
Áth na mBreo	the ford across the River Boyne at Brú na Bóinne
bastún	a fool or stupid person
Béal Átha na Sluaigh	literally 'the Approach to the Ford of the Multitude': modern Ballinasloe
Béal Ború	large ring-fort at southern end of Lough Derg, just north of Killaloe
Beann Éadair	modern Howth
banshee (bean sí)	literally 'fairy woman': otherworldly announcer of impending death
bodach	a rough, ignorant person
boreen (bóithrín)	a narrow by-road
Bran	one of Fionn Mac Cumhail's dogs
breac	the sleep found in your eyes just after waking
Breas	a mythical king of the Tuatha Dé Danann
Brosnach	literally 'broken firewood': modern Brosna, a village in north-east Kerry
cailleach	a hag
cáis	cheese
capall	a horse
carraig	a rock

céilí	an evening or night-time gathering for conversation, music and dancing
Ciarraí	modern Kerry
Clanna Buí	Clandeboy, County Antrim
cluas	an ear
Coill Cham	literally 'the Crooked Wood'
Corca Baiscinn	a district in west Clare
Corca Dhuibhne	the Dingle peninsula
Croagh Dhubh	literally 'the Black Mountain'
Crom	ancient idol having his dwelling at Magh Sléacht, County Cavan
Dagda	'the Good God': one of the Tuatha Dé Danann, father of Aongus an Bhrogha
Dál nAraidhe	an area in south Antrim whose people, with the Ulaidh, are regarded as the true Ulstermen
Danu	ancient Celtic goddess
Dhera!	a word used to express disbelief or indifference
dób buí	yellow clay
dób dearg	red clay
Doire Fhada	literally 'the long oak-wood'
Doire Olc	literally 'the evil or inhospitable oak-wood'
donáinín	a weak, miserable person
draíocht	magic
draoi	a druid
Dubhat	Dowth, north-east of Newgrange, on the River Boyne
Dubhdraoi	literally 'Black Druid'
Dún	a fortified dwelling or princely residence
Dún Ailinne	a royal enclosure in County Kildare
Dún Mór	literally 'the Big Fort'
Eamhain Macha	ancient capital of Ulster; modern Navan Fort, near Armagh City
fáilte	welcome
féile	a feast
Fianna Éireann	the army of warriors led by Fionn Mac Cumhail
Firbolg	one of the peoples of ancient Ireland
Fir Rois	the ancient inhabitants of the area corresponding to modern east Monaghan and Louth
gallán	a standing stone

gamal	a stupid person
gath	a spear
An Gath Dearg	the Red Spear
Gleann na nGealt	literally 'the Glen of the Mad': modern Glenagalt, near Camp, County Kerry
gruama	gloomy
Inbhear Scéine	Kenmare Bay
Íseal brí	low spirits, depression
Lá Bealtaine	May Day
leacht	a memorial stone or gravestone
Leacht na nUasal	the Gravestone of the Noble Ones
Leath Choinn	the northern half of Ireland
Leath Mogha	the southern half of Ireland
Linn na bPúcaí	literally 'the Pool of the Dark Spirits'
Lios Liath	literally 'the Grey Fort'
Lios na gCearrbhach	literally 'the Fort of the Gamblers': modern Lisburn, County Antrim
Loch Cam	literally 'the Crooked Lake': modern Camlough, County Armagh
Loch Neacach	Lough Neagh
Lugh	Celtic god of light and genius
Maigh Chuilinn	literally 'the Plain of Holly': modern Moycullen, County Galway
Maighnis	Fionn Mac Cumhail's wife
maor	a steward
maslach	insulting
Modh díreach	the direct way
Ochón!	an interjection of grief: 'Alas!', 'Woe!'
Olagón ó!	an interjection of grief: 'Alas!'
piseog	an evil charm or spell to take away a person's luck
plámás	flattery, soft talk
poitín	home-distilled liquor
poll	hole
Poll Buí	literally 'the Yellow Hole'
pusachán	a whiner or complainer
ráiméis	nonsense
rann	a verse of a poem or song
Ráth Croghan	Cruachain, County Roscommon, capital of ancient Connaught

Reacaire	a reciter of stories or verse
Ros na Rí	literally 'the Wood of the Kings': Rosnaree, a ford of the River Boyne near Newgrange
ruaille buaille	confused noise
Samhain	the first day of winter, 1 November
Sceolaing	one of Fionn's dogs
seanchaí	a teller of old tales
seilmide	a snail
shebeen (síbín)	an illicit public house
Sídh Cnogbha	Knowth, north-west of Newgrange, on the River Boyne
Sídh i mBroga	Newgrange
síógaí	the fairies
Sliabh Bladhma	Slieve Bloom, in Counties Laois and Offaly
Sliabh Bregha	near Mellifont, County Louth
Sliabh Luachra	area on the border of Kerry and Cork, around Rathmore and Ballydesmond
Slí na Fírinne	literally 'the Way of Truth': death
steall	a draught of liquid
súlach	dirty, unpleasant liquid
súnc	a heavy blow
Teamhair Luachra	literally 'the Tara (assembly hill) of Sliabh Luachra', said by some to be the height called 'the Moats' in Brosna, County Kerry
tiarna	lord
Tuatha Dé Danann	literally 'the people of the goddess Dana'
Uladh	Ulster

NOTES

1.   cf. 'The Druid of Feakle's Tooth Shop' in *Humorous Irish Tales for Children* (Mercier Press, 1998).

2   Ibid.

3   Ibid.

4.   cf. 'The Dream Hour' in *Gruesome Irish Tales for Children* (Mercier Press, 1997).